# TalkTalk

**A children's book author
speaks to grown-ups.**

## Also by E. L. Konigsburg

# TalkTalk

**A children's book author
speaks to grown-ups.**

E. L. Konigsburg

A JEAN KARL BOOK

ATHENEUM

ATHENEUM
An imprint of Simon & Schuster Children's Publishing Division
1230 Avenue of the Americas
New York, NY 10020

Designed by Ann Bobco and Anne Scatto
The text of this book is set in Perpetua.

First edition
Printed in the United States of America
10  9  8  7  6  5  4  3  2  1

Library of Congress Cataloging-in-Publication Data
Konigsburg, E. L.
    TalkTalk / E. L. Konigsburg.
    p.  cm.
    "A Jean Karl Book."
    ISBN 0-689-31993-2
    1. Konigsburg, E. L.—Authorship.  2. Children's stories, American—History and criticism—
Theory, etc.  3.Children's stories—Authorship.  4. Children—Books and reading.  I. Title.
II. Title: TalkTalk.
PS3561.O459Z475  1995
810.9'9282—dc20            94-32341  CIP

IMO Mo

# Contents

# Acknowledgments

Jean Karl's advice to make the whole more than the sum of its parts by linking the speeches to one another proved to be the insightful incentive that made me look forward and back to see these speeches in a new light. I thank her first for that. And I thank her, too, for the research she did, the letters—worldwide—she wrote, and the contacts she made to obtain permissions for printing the pictures that illustrate three of these speeches. I thank Jon Lanman for being the consistent voice in the corner office during several changes of the guard. I thank Ann Bobco for her inspired art direction, her optimism, and our lengthy working conversations over long distance with her saying, "We're almost there." I thank Patricia Buckley for being a friend in the home office.

I also want to thank three friends not in the office: Colette Coman for translating French; Jack Dreher for translating Italian; and Judith Viorst for a phone call, made immediately after reading my manuscript, telling me the baby has all its fingers and all its toes and was born speaking.

I thank Sarah Mitchell at Art Resource for her interest and her help in finding suitable transparencies of artwork from medieval to modern. I thank Evan Levine of the Education Department of the Metropolitan Museum of Art for putting me in contact with Beatrice Epstein of their Photo Slide Library, who tracked down the elusive picture of the stucco and plaster *Bust of a Lady* that the museum purchased in 1965. I thank Anne Scatto for fitting the pieces on the pages and Howard Kaplan for keeping track of the pieces.

My husband, David, who is mentioned several times in the course of these speeches, must be mentioned here, too, for I can never consider complete a list of people to thank without including his name. I thank him for tuning in when he should and tuning out when he should. It is he who hears the hollering and halting, the screeching and screaming before the work has the spirit of *sprezzatura*.

Last, I want to thank all the people in the auditoriums, cafetoriums, media centers, and public rooms of Holiday Inns who have listened to what I have had to say about children and books and who have said that they would like to read what they had heard. They are my audience: lovers of print on paper.

# TalkTalk

**A children's book author
speaks to grown-ups.**

# Talk and Talk

When I delivered the first of these speeches at the annual convention of the American Library Association in 1968, I was the mother of three. I have since become the grandmother of five. Having shifted my generation, I have, by definition, shifted my point of view. I could say that like an old lady without bifocals, I must hold the printed page at arm's length just to make it possible to read. I could say that. But I won't. Instead I choose to think of myself as the viewer of a large Impressionist painting standing back—and farther back—to see all those dabs of color come into focus. I see myself moving deeper into the work by standing farther back from it.

First to last, these speeches reflect or reflect upon the changes in children's literature in the United States over the past quarter century. The change overriding all others is growth. In a letter dated July 7, 1993, Judy V. Wilson, former president and general manager of the Children's Book Group of Macmillan Publishing Company wrote, "[I]n 1980 2800 children's books were published and in 1988 5000 a year. I don't have more recent numbers but it could be a 50% increase in the past five years."

Growth certainly means greater numbers, but it also

means development from a simpler to a more complex form, and publishing children's books has certainly grown more complex.

When my first book was published in the spring of 1967, Atheneum was a small independent publisher with offices in an old brownstone on East Thirty-eighth Street. There was a big red letter *A* on the door. The Children's Book Department was on the fifth floor—walk-up. Jean Karl was its founder and editor.

Books were published twice a year—spring and fall—to little fanfare and quiet profit. The major steps for getting a children's novel into the hands of a child were: a writer wrote it; an editor accepted it; a publisher published it; a director of library services sent the book to the media and major library systems for review; the book was purchased by schools and libraries; children read it.

Children's books stayed on the shelves a long time. Recency and primacy comfortably coexisted. Books went into third, fourth—fortieth—reprintings. The backlist books, those for which all the editorial and start-up costs had already been paid, were the backbone of the children's book departments. Experimentation, excitement, lay in the front list; pride and profitability, in the back.

In 1979 Atheneum merged with Scribner's. Macmillan bought Atheneum-Scribner's in 1984. Maxwell bought Macmillan in 1988. Until February 1994, when Paramount bought Maxwell Macmillan, Atheneum was one of nine imprints of the Macmillan Children's Book Group. Paramount, which also owns Simon & Schuster, has designed its children's book group as follows: three trade hardcover imprints, one paperback imprint, and an imprint that will publish novelty-merchandise items. In July 1994, Viacom bought Paramount, but we don't have to talk about that. As the corporate structure now stands, Atheneum will be one of the three Simon & Schuster hardcover imprints; it will absorb Scribner's.

In the last rounds of corporate buyouts, the children's book departments were part of the dowry. They weren't the vast estates of the reference and textbook divisions or the many mansions of adult trade books, they were the small, beautifully wrought silver tea service that had been in the family for years, carried down from the attic, brought to the bargaining table, polished and still holding water–flavored water.

—✦—

When I step back to see the patterns of growth in the publishing of children's books, I find that I can tease out trends–those sustained streaks of color that at various times are applied to subject matter, style, and/or genre of what is published.

A current trend in children's book publishing is the increased role of marketing. Tracking the role that marketing has played can show how growth means development from a simpler to a more complex form. Growth has affected the marketing of children's books, and marketing, in turn, has affected growth.

Complications in marketing started even before the corporate mergers. When Atheneum Books for Children was a fifth-floor walk-up, over 95 percent of children's trade books were sold to schools and public libraries. To present its books to the market, children's book departments had a small department of library services, which sent copies of the books to professional journals and major library systems for review. Spring and fall, they put together catalogs of the lists and set up ads in trade publications. They also arranged attendance and entertainment at library and education conferences so that people in publishing could meet people who bought books. The director of library services reported to the children's book editor.

In the late 1960s and early 1970s, when the population of

the United States shifted toward the Sunbelt, new schools were being built with media centers integral to their construction. The new configurations and the increased numbers of school libraries improved the market for children's trade books as well as textbooks. At the same time that school libraries were developing into healthy markets for trade books, the federal government started funneling money into school libraries as part of its Great Society programs, and the publishing world experienced the first great swelling in the number of children's books needed to satisfy the market. Large school systems developed their own selection processes, and the continental divide in opinion drifted West and South along with the shift of population. Directors of library services were now covering education and reading conferences as well as library conferences in states from coast to coast.

When Atheneum was a brownstone, and I was a pup, paperback children's books were an egg. Five years later, the egg hatched. And five years after that, paperbacks were fully feathered and had taken off. The emergence of paperbacks, coupled with an educational trend toward using trade books instead of basal readers, allowed schools to purchase classroom sets of books.

Strange as it may seem, bookstores did not become a viable market for children's books until some time after the federal money for school libraries dried up, and the publishers, newly incorporated by the first of the mergers, wooed the bookstore market to make up the loss of Great Society funds. The children's section in many had been (many still are) more gift department than book department. In the mid-1970s, after paperbacks had gained a foothold in children's books, bookstores began to stock books other than Nancy Drew, novelty items, and mass-market books, and stores devoted exclusively to children's books started up in suburban strip malls and on city sidewalks.

Directors of library services now had to attend to book-store needs.

Corporate mergers increased the number of imprints a single publisher would market; paperbacks increased the kinds of books to be marketed. The improved school library market, the new importance of bookstores, and the good old standby public library market—everything and everyone needing goodwill—complicated the role of the department of library services. The staff grew and developed specialties such as catalog design, conference planning, sales conferences, and author appearances. The department of library services became the marketing department, and its director no longer reported to the editor but took his seat at the conference table beside the children's book editor and the publisher.

The increased role of marketing in the publishing of children's books has resulted in marketing's sharing or shading a publishing decision. Not always, but sometimes. A single two-part scenario, in which I played a role, will demonstrate how this sometimes happens and how it sometimes doesn't.

It is summer. It is late ante meridiem. We are doing brunch. My host is a children's book editor. She is a recent hire of a large publishing house with a West Coast presence. This is the West Coast. This is where right-on-red came from. This is L.A., the city where the phone is a prosthesis. She asks if we can do a deal. I know she means a book. I tell her I've been thinking about a book. This book will be a picture book. My second grandchild will be a character. I have a title: *Amy Elizabeth Explores Bloomingdale's*. She expresses enthusiasm. We part, mellowed out on champagne and promise.

I submit the manuscript. I do not receive a reply—not even an acknowledgment of receipt—for more than a month. *Uh-oh*.

Experience has taught me that when a response to a requested manuscript is long in coming, the manuscript is in trouble. I was right. What experience had not prepared me for, however, was the source of the problem. In her letter, the editor wrote:

> What confuses me however, is that the title is misleading, and I think the reaction of *sales reps and booksellers* [italics mine] will be negative rather than positive. The book is about something completely different than the title suggests and I think the reader will ultimately be disappointed. It seems to me that it could be called AMY ELIZABETH TRIES TO EXPLORE BLOOMINGDALE'S or AMY ELIZABETH DOESN'T EXPLORE BLOOMINGDALE'S or perhaps more clever than the above that conveys to the reader that the book will be satisfying even if you don't get to go to Bloomingdale's. I also think that *reviewers* [italics mine] would object to the book disappointing the child.

We could not agree on a treatment for the book, and I requested that she return the manuscript to me. I then submitted it to Jean Karl, who has been my forever editor. Her letter, talking about the same book, said:

> . . . The idea of setting out for someplace and never getting there—but seeing a good many other places along the way—is always amusing. However, somehow . . . the text . . . sits on the surface of events in a way that does not bring the reader fully into the experience.

The difference in these two criticisms points out the difference between market-driven and book-driven publishing. Jean Karl trusts her own taste and judgment to find books that will satisfy the marketplace. She trusts something else, too: she trusts her writers. Her criticism of my manuscript shows that she trusted me to rework the text in a way that would bring the reader in, for that was the real problem with the book. Subsequent to its publication (October 1992) not one *reviewer, bookseller, or librarian* [italics mine] has objected to the title.

—✦—

Sometimes trends affect genre. Genres, though seeming replete and powerful for a time, fade away and sometimes disappear, affecting the pattern but not changing the direction of growth in children's books.

In the years since I walked up four flights of stairs to reach the Atheneum Children's Book Department, I have seen young adult novels grow breasts and hair and then stop short of further growth. I have seen series books spawn healthy litters, one after another. Even as I write, I see picture books fighting for room at the trough while chapter books are being nursed to great good health.

Trends start, swell, and disappear but leave their mark, a protrusion on the forward thrust. Fads, on the other hand, arrive quickly, take over, and disappear as suddenly as they appeared. Being short-lived, they are swept along within a trend and alter, only briefly, its texture.

Fads infect subject matter and genre, and while they are in full blossom, they are so ubiquitous that it is hard to believe that they will pass, but they do. In this past quarter century, I have seen Batman come and go and come and go again. Ninja Turtles: here, there, everywhere–yesterday. Trolls have come and gone and come and–as of this morning–are on the deeply discounted table at Kmart.

When a fad influences a genre, we get *choose-your-own-adventure* books, the hula hoops of the eighties.

The current fad in marketing is the celebrity-authored children's book. Whoopi Goldberg, Jamie Lee Curtis, Dom

Deluise, actors; Olivia Newton-John, singer; the Simons, Carly and Paul, songwriters and singers; and Fergie, an English duchess, have all contributed to recent children's books lists. Dolly Parton has one "in development." My friend, the poet, essayist, and children's book author Judith Viorst, explained, "Children's books have become the designer perfume of the nineties."

It was inevitable, I suppose, that when the entertainment industry married into the publishing family, they would want children of their very own. They did not produce books, however. They produced book-products. Novelizations. Of movies, of TV shows. Even song lyrics. Biographies that are rushed to print before their subjects' fifteen minutes of fame have run out are also book-products. So, too, are headline stories that are rushed from talk-show circuit to printing press. Authors of book-products are now thought of as "content providers." Time will tell if the metamorphosis from producing a book into manufacturing book-products will or will not be a trend. I fear one and hope the other.

—+—

While each of my books has been written because I had a story I wanted to tell, these speeches were written because I had something I wanted to say. The audience for the former is children; for the latter, adults. Much more than my books, these speeches reflect or reflect upon what has been going on in the world of children's literature at the time they were written. I recognize—with a measure of amused detachment—that some were written as a reaction to trends; others, to fads.

These speeches are presented in the order in which they were written. I have given these talks in cafetoriums, auditoriums, and the public rooms of Holiday Inns. Even though I have not always been on a stage when addressing an audience, I have tried to set the stage. Between talk and talk, I have written passages connecting the speeches to the time in which they were written and to one another. And that is *TalkTalk*.

—+—

In *Up From Jericho Tel,* I tried to explore the gifts it takes to succeed in the arts. One is *timing.* I believe that if I had written *Jennifer, Hecate, Macbeth, William McKinley and Me, Elizabeth* twelve years before I did, it would not have been published. The time to broaden the base of allowable subject matter coincided with the publication of this, my first book. In my Newbery address, I talk about this first mark of growth in the field of literature for children.

# 1. Newbery Award Acceptance

You see before you today a grateful convert from chemistry. Grateful that I converted and grateful that you have labeled the change successful. The world of chemistry, too, is thankful; it is a neater and safer place since I left. This conversion was not so difficult as some others I have gone through. The transformation from smoker into nonsmoker was far more difficult, and the change from high-school-graduate-me into girl-chemist-me was more revolutionary. My writing is not a conversion, really, but a reversion, a reversion to type. A chemist needs symbols and equations, and a chemist needs test tubes and the exact metric measure. A chemist needs this equipment, but I do not. I can go for maybe even five whole days without thinking about gram molecular weights. But not words. I think about words a lot. I need words. I need written-down, black-on-white, printed words. Let me count the ways.

There was a long newspaper strike the first winter we moved into metropolitan New York. Saturday used to be my day off, and I used that day for taking art lessons in the morning and for exploring Manhattan in the afternoon. Our suburbs were New Jersey suburbs then, and my last piece of walking involved a cross-town journey toward the Port Authority Bus Terminal. On one of those Saturdays, as I was in the heart of the theater district, a volley of teen-age girls came larruping down the street bellowing, "The Rolling Stones! The Rolling Stones!" Up ahead, a small bunch of long-haired boys broke into a run and ducked into an alley, Shubert Alley. The girls pursued, and the Rolling Stones gathered; they pushed their collective hair out of their collective eyes and signed autographs.

I told my family about this small happening when I came home, but that was not enough. The next day I wanted to show them an account of it in the paper. But there was no Sunday paper then. It didn't get written down. I had seen it happen, and still I missed its not being written down. Even now, I miss its never having been written down. I need to see the words to make more real that which I have experienced. And that is the first way I need words. A quotation from my old world of science explains it: ontogeny recapitulates phylogeny. Each animal in its individual development passes through stages in which it resembles its remote ancestors. I spread words on paper for the same reasons that Cro-Magnon man spread pictures on the walls of caves. I need to see it put down: the Rolling Stones and the squealing girls. Thus, first of all, writing it down adds another dimension to reality and satisfies an atavistic need.

And I need words for a second reason. I need them for the reasons that Jane Austen probably did. She told about the dailiness of living. She presented a picture that only someone both involved with her times and detached from them could present. Just like me. I am involved in the everyday, corn-flakes, worn-out-sneakers way of life of my children; yet I am detached from it by several decades. And I give words to the supermarket shopping and to the laundromat just as Jane Austen gave words to afternoon visiting and worry about drafts from open windows.

Just as she stood in a corridor, sheltered by roof and walls from the larger world of her century, just as she stood there and described what was happening in the cubicles of civilization, I stand in my corridor. My corridor is my generation, a hallway away from the children that I breed and need and write about. I peek into homes sitting on quarter-acre lots and into apartments with two bedrooms and two baths. So I need words for this reason: to make a record of a place, suburban America, and a time, early autumn of the twentieth century.

My phylogenetic need, adding another dimension to reality, and my class and order need, making record, are certainly the wind at my back, but a family need is the directed, strong gust that pushes me to my desk. And here I don't mean *family* in the taxonomic sense. I mean *family* that I lived in when I was growing up and *family* that I live in now.

Read *Mary Poppins,* and you get a good glimpse of upper-middle-class family life in England a quarter of a century ago, a family that had basis in fact. Besides Mary there were Cook and Robertson Ay, and Ellen to lay the table. The outside of the Banks house needed paint. Would such a household exist in a middle-class neighborhood in a Shaker Heights, Ohio, or a Paramus, New Jersey? Hardly. There would be no cook; mother would be subscribing to *Gourmet* magazine. Robertson Ay's salary would easily buy the paint, and Mr. Banks would be cleaning the leaves out of his gutters on a Sunday afternoon. No one in the Scarsdales of this country allows the house to get run down. It is not in the order of things to purchase services instead of paint.

Read *The Secret Garden,* and you find another world that I know about only in words. Here is a family living on a large estate staffed by servants who are devoted to the two generations living there. Here is a father who has no visible source of income. He neither reaps nor sows; he doesn't even commute. He apparently never heard of permissiveness in raising children. He travels around Europe in search of himself, and no one resents his leaving his family to do it. Families of this kind had a basis in fact, but fact remote from me.

I have such faith in words that when I read about such families as a child, I thought that they were the norm and that the way I lived was subnormal, waiting for normal.

Where were the stories then about growing up in a small mill town where there was no one named Jones in your class? Where were the stories that made having a class full of Radasevitches and Gabellas and Zaharious normal? There were stories about the crowd meeting at the corner drugstore after school. Where were the stories that told about the store owner closing his place from 3:15 until 4:00 p.m. because he found that what he gained in sales of Coca-Cola he lost in stolen Hershey Bars? How come that druggist never seemed normal to me? He was supposed to be grumpy but lovable; the stories of my time all said so.

Where are the stories now about fathers who come home from work grouchy? Not mean. Not mad. Just nicely, mildly grouchy. Where are the words that tell about mothers who are just slightly hungover on the morning after New Year's Eve? Not drunkard mothers. Just headachey ones. Where are the stories that tell about the pushy ladies? Not real social climbers. Just moderately pushy. Where are all the parents who are experts on schools? They are all around me in the suburbs of New Jersey and New York, in Pennsylvania and Florida, too. Where are they in books? Some of them are in my books.

And I put them there for my kids. To excuse myself to my kids. Because I have this foolish faith in words. Because I want to show it happening. Because for some atavistic, artistic, inexplicable reason, I believe that the writing of it makes normal of it.

Some of the words come from another family part of me. From being a mother. From the part of me that urges, "Say something else, too. Describe, sure, describe what life is like in these suburbs. Tell how it is normal to be very comfortable on the outside but very uncomfortable on the inside. Tell how funny it all is. But tell a little something else, too. What can it hurt? Tell a little something else—about how you can be a nonconformist and about how you can be an outsider. And tell how you are entitled to a little privacy. But for goodness' sake, say all that very softly. Let the telling be like fudge-ripple ice cream. You keep licking vanilla, but every now and then you come to something darker and deeper and with a stronger flavor. Let the something-else words be the chocolate."

The illustrations probably come from the kindergartener who lives inside, somewhere inside me, who says, "Silly, don't you know that it is called *show and tell?* Hold up and show and then tell." I have to show how Mrs. Frankweiler looks and how Jennifer looks. Besides, I like to draw, and I like to complete things, and doing the illustrations answers these simple needs.

And that is my metamorphosis; I guess it was really that and not a conversion at all. The egg that gives form to the caterpillar and then to the chrysalis was really meant to be a butterfly in the first place. Chemistry was my larval stage, and those nine years at home doing diaper service were my cocoon. And you see standing before you today the moth I was always meant to be. (Well, I hardly qualify as a butter-fly.) A moth who lives on words.

On January 13, after I had finished doing my Zorba Dance and after I had cried over the phone to Mae Durham and to Jean Karl, after I had said all the *I can't believe it's* and all the *Oh, no, not really's,* I turned to my husband and asked a typical-wife question, "Did you ever think fifteen years ago when you married a li'l ole organic chemist from Farrell, Pennsylvania, that you were marrying a future Newbery winner and run-ner-up?" And my husband answered in typical-David fashion, "No, but I knew it would be a nice day when it happened."

And it was a nice day. It's been a whole row of wonderful days since it happened. Thank you, Jean Karl, for helping to give Jennifer and Elizabeth and Claudia and Jamie that all-important extra dimension, print on paper. Thank you, Mae Durham and all the members of the committee, for deciding that my words were special. And thank you, Mr. Melcher, for the medal that stamps them special. All of you, thank you, for giving me something that allows me to go home like Claudia—different on the inside where it counts.

# Those 60s

**B**roadening the base of allowable subject matter in children's literature preceded broadening the base of allowable language. It has always been so. In *The Sun Also Rises* by Ernest Hemingway, the narrator, Jake Barnes, alludes to a war injury that makes him unable to help him and Lady Ashley get rid of their pimples. In chapter 4, Jake makes his most direct reference to his injury:

> Well, it was a rotten way to be wounded and flying on a joke front like the Italian. In the Italian hospital we were going to form a society. It had a funny name in Italian.

Had Hemingway published *The Sun Also Rises* in 1994 instead of 1926, no one would have had to guess the nature of Jake Barnes's injury or look up the funny name in Italian. In the summer of 1993 Lorena Bobbitt (real name, real person) cut off her husband's penis, and every respectable newspaper in the country said so. The "funny name in Italian" is *senzapene*.

Show always precedes tell.

Take the story of the publication of two children's books: *The Secret River,* a 1956 Newbery Honor Book by Marjorie

Kinnan Rawlings and my own novel, *Jennifer, Hecate, Macbeth, William McKinley and Me, Elizabeth,* a 1968 Newbery Honor Book.

Several years after Atheneum Publishers had merged with Scribner's, two friends and I visited Ms. Rawlings's home in Cross Creek, Florida. I mentioned to the guide that I and one of the gentlemen I was with were associated with Scribner's, Ms. Rawlings's publisher, and that we were involved with children's books.

The guide took out a copy of *The Secret River,* the only children's story that Rawlings ever wrote. She mentioned that Mr. Scribner had thought of an ingenious way to circumvent any reader resistance to the fact that the story's heroine, Calpurnia, was black. He had the book printed on brown paper.

As originally written, the manuscript of *Jennifer, Hecate, Macbeth,William McKinley and Me, Elizabeth* made no mention of the fact that Jennifer, one of the protagonists in the story, is black. Not because I wanted to circumvent the issue but because I wanted to show how unimportant race was to the friendship that develops between her and the narrator, Elizabeth. I had submitted a sample set of illustrations that clearly showed that Jennifer was, indeed, black.

In a letter dated January 20, 1966, ten years after Rawlings's *The Secret River* was named a Newbery Honor Book, Jean Karl wrote:

> There are a few minor questions that need answering . . . Why, for example, if Jennifer is a Negro does the text not say so. Elizabeth is forthright enough to be casual about it, I would think.

I agreed that if Jennifer's color were to be truly unimportant—except that it marked her as an outsider—it would be an affectation not to mention that she was black, so I slipped a reference into the story in a place where it would further detail Jennifer's outsiderness.

The difference between printing Calpurnia's story of *The Secret River* on brown paper and portraying a black heroine in *Jennifer, Hecate, Macbeth, William McKinley and Me, Elizabeth* marks an important change that has taken place in the world of children's books.

When my book was published in 1967, I used the term *Negro* for that single reference. In the mid-1970s when the book was being reprinted, I requested that the word be changed to *black*. If I were writing the story today, I would use the term *African-American*. The choice of terms is a reflection of the current cultural trend. However, I shall not request another change. Twenty-five years from now I trust readers will see my use of *black* as the local color of the times.

Words do, indeed, add a dimension to reality, for they are the artifacts of a civilization. But language—language—is a form of behavior.

Language reflects culture.

Today's language inevitably reflects the omnipresence of television. I am not concerned with the appearance of fad phrases—*Cowabunga! Dy-no-mite!* or Kiss my grits—but I am concerned with writing that attempts to reflect contemporary culture by imitating the dialogue patterns on TV. It is called "Waiting for the Punchline."

Here is the formula: A says $a^1$; B says $b^1$; A says $a^2$; B delivers put-down. Sometimes another put-down follows. Sometimes they escalate. The dialogue on TV is delivered with body language and canned laughter. Books have to deliver without shtick.

Since language is the only tool with which writers can reflect and shape a culture, it must be transformed into art. Language is not a limitation on the art of literature; it is a glorification. It has been the scaffolding inside which nations and philosophies have been built, and the language of literature has added the ornamental pediment by which the culture is remembered.

—✝—

In a speech that I call "Lethal Weapon" I talk about language shaping one's thinking. I wrote this speech in the fall following my Newbery address and have revised it several times since. The first major revision came about after a trip to China in 1980. I couldn't imagine doing library research, as the Chinese must, without an alphabet. (Mao Zedong himself had once been a librarian at the University of Beijing.)

"How do you file anything?" I asked our Chinese guide. "How do you look something up in a dictionary?" I asked. It took several explanations before I could be convinced that indexing could be done at all. That is only one way that language shapes a person's thinking. Imagine having to learn a language that conveys not just shades of meaning but whole different meanings by using different tones. Wouldn't that also shape the way you listen?

As we moved through the seventies and eighties, I have revised the references I used in this speech. I have brought the slang and the slogans up to date, for slang and slogans are fads, but what has happened to the language in children's books is change. As presented here, "Lethal Weapon" is the most recent version of the speech I wrote about my respect for, love of, need for, and delight in language.

# 2. Lethal Weapon

Not too long ago, a certain distant relative of mine told me that I ought to buy a word processor. She said, "Just think how much better you would write, darling, if you had one. In your line of work, my dear, you ought to have the best possible tools." I told her that I had a word processor, and she said, "Oh," and asked me if in my line of work, it was tax deductible.

With some relatives you can't explain anything that is not tax deductible, so I made no effort to explain to this person that the computer that sits on top of my desk is, indeed, tax deductible, but the best possible tool in my line of work is not.

My IBM PC does, indeed, process words. It can process them into columns; it can fill pages with X's and O's; it can cut and splice sentences or even whole paragraphs and rearrange them, and when I write, I use many of these processes, and I find them useful, but the computer is not my best possible tool.

The best possible tool of my line of work is the word processor that lies not in the middle of my desk but in the left side of my brain, for it is the brain and not the IBM PC that processes words into language.

It is language that is the basic tool of my trade, and it is language—words processed into language—that I would like to explore with you.

I love language. I speak no foreign tongue, so I must qualify that statement to: I love the English language. It is a good language to love. It is—well—so American. I think it is more American than it is English.

First of all, the English language developed from the Anglo-Saxons, the people who were conquered by William the Conqueror, and who were considered the lower classes. From 1066 until about the time of the invention of the printing press, Norman French was the language of the aristocracy in England. The lower classes gave birth to English, and because it is a blend of many dialects it has lost the refined declensions of the Romance languages. We have a paucity of verb and noun endings in English, and I find that blurring of differences to be very American. Americans—much more than the English—are always filing away at marginal differentiations. The office secretary and office executive both dress for success, and the Chevrolet used to try to look like a Cadillac, and nowadays, the Cadillac tries to look like a Chevy.

The English language has more borrowed words than any other language—just like the borrowed cuisines in the restaurants of any large American city. English has a larger vocabulary than any other language—one-third larger than French, I believe—and that, too, is American. Bigness is American.

English is vigorous because of its peasant roots. Take the matter of food. It is calf on the hoof, but veal on the table. Ox in the pasture, beef on the table. Sheep in the meadow, mutton on the table. Calf, ox, and sheep are all of Old English derivation; veal, beef, and mutton are from the Old French. The peasants handled it on the hoof; the Normans at table. House comes from Old English; mansion from the French. That part of the English language derived from its less refined sources is not only rougher but more colorful, too. Just like the American people. Gut is a word with more punch than intestine. Gut is of Middle English derivation and so is groan, and so is groin. And so, too, are many of our more famous four-lettered words. Both the f-word and the sh-word derive from the Anglo-Saxon.

I love the English language. I think we should consider ourselves lucky to have it as our native tongue.

Where would we be without it?

But worse, where would we be without language altogether?

The Pyramids, the smile of the Mona Lisa, say many things to many people, but when people want to tell you what they mean, or how they got there, they resort to language.

Man is the only species to have a culture, and he has a culture only because he has a language.

It is language that separates man from beast, and it all started with Adam. God did not name the animals. He let Adam do it. Genesis, chapter 2, verses 19 and 20:

> . . . the Lord God formed every beast of the field, and every fowl of the air; and brought them unto the man to see what he would call them; and whatsoever the man would call every living creature, that was to be the name thereof. And the man gave names to all cattle, and to the fowl of the air, and to every beast of the field.

Other animals can have a tradition—rats transmit to one another a knowledge of poisons; a monkey can teach all of his relatives and friends how to clean potatoes and even how to salt them by dipping them into salt water. He can teach a whole population how to salt potatoes, but his transmission of that knowledge is dependent upon the presence of the potato and the salt water. The monkey can show, but he cannot tell.

He cannot tell because he does not have the gift of language.

Mark Twain said, "I believe that our Heavenly Father invented man because He was disappointed in the monkey." I believe God invented man because She wanted someone to talk to.

Man may be a naked ape. Certainly, he is that. But that is not all he is. He is more. The ape is surely in man, but man is nowhere at all in the ape. Because the ape does not have language, and man does. Words as symbols, words as servants of conceptual thinking, belong to man and to man alone. Not to the ape, not to the elephant, not to your cocker spaniel who can let you know he wants to go out and can let you know when he is hungry. Language does not even belong to the parrot who can say she wants a cracker. Polly may say she wants a cracker, but she is like that word processor sitting on top of my desk at home; she has been programmed to say she wants one, and she does not know—any more than my PC knows—what the hell she is asking for.

*Hell* is another good four-lettered Anglo-Saxon word.

Polly has the words, but she does not have language. Contrast Polly with Marlee Matlin. When Marlee Matlin, who is deaf, wanted to tell a television audience how she felt about winning an Oscar for her performance in *Children of a Lesser God,* she used sign language. The following year when she was presenting an award, she spoke, but her first communication was every bit as moving and successful as her second because in both cases—signing and speaking—she used the symbols of language.

Language makes it possible to maintain a tradition independent of environment. We can tell our children how to salt a potato because we have a word symbol for salt and for potato and action verbs to tell what to do with each.

With language something new came into the world: immortality of thought and immortality of knowledge.

An entire race can perish, but their culture—their recipe for salting potatoes—can stay alive in libraries. We can see

Stonehenge, but we must guess at how it got there and why. Because stones are not words. Stonehenge remains much more isolated in our collective cultural consciousness than the Pyramids—which were built at the same time. Why? Because we have no words to connect the builders' philosophy with their temple. But in the Pyramids there are indeed sermons in stones, and archaeologists have uncovered the language that keeps the thought and the philosophy behind them alive. And that is why the Bible, the Old Testament, has been a more pervasive monument than either the Pyramids or Stonehenge: it is made of material stronger and more durable and more portable than stone—language.

It is language that truly reflects a nation.

On a recent return flight from Australia, I found a magazine called *ITA* that is published in Australia. In it appeared an article about a young woman named Heather Glass, who spent four years at the Tokyo University of Foreign Studies and who became a language consultant for her state government. Japan is Australia's principal trading partner. In the short article, Heather is quoted: "The Japanese have no word for truth. They say: 'Don't do that, you'll be seen,' rather than 'don't do that, it's wrong.'"

I was shocked. When I read, "The Japanese have no word for truth," I asked myself, Have we sold Rockefeller Center to a nation that has no word for truth? Is Saks Fifth Avenue now owned by a people who do not know a true Louis Vuitton bag from a fake? Has Hollywood, our chief maker of images, sold out to a nation that has no word for truth? I couldn't believe that a whole society exists, can possibly exist, without a word for truth. In a court of law, don't the Japanese swear to tell the truth, the whole truth, and nothing but the truth? How can a nation exist without a word for a concept that is at the core of our system of justice? Truth is more than the core; it is the whole apple.

So I wrote to Mrs. Okamoto, the woman who translates some of my books into Japanese. I sent her a copy of the article, and I asked, "Can it be true that the Japanese have no word for truth?" How's that for asking a dumb question? Isn't that a lot like shouting to a person who cannot hear?

Mrs. Okamoto answered by return mail. Here is part of her letter:

> As for your question . . . I understand what you say about the word 'the truth' and we Japanese do have the word the truth. I don't know why this person Heather says such ridiculous thing!! . . . we have the belief and thought and idea and conception and words for THE TRUTH! SHINJITSU, or SHIRI, or MAKO TO etc. How can we live without the truth??! I even feel angry when I read the part–They say: 'Don't do that, you'll be seen,' rather than 'Don't do that, it's wrong.' That's wrong!!! Big mistake!! I think it's almost insulting Japanese. We believe that if we do something wrong, even if nobody knows or sees, we must go to Hell after the death!! Believe me, please!

Mrs. Okamoto's defense against the assassination attempt made on the Japanese character by Heather Glass is heated and righteous. Language can join nations or separate them. Language is not just a tool of the writing trade; in politics and business, it can be a lethal weapon. A hundred years ago, Oscar Wilde said, "We have really everything in common with America nowadays, except, of course, language."

In his *New York* magazine review (April 29, 1991) of *Daddy Nostalgia,* a movie in which Dirk Bogarde plays the title character, a spoiled British businessman who has fallen ill, David Denby cites a particular scene where Daddy Nostalgia says to his daughter that life was "sweeter when there was servants." I noted that he was not quoted as saying that life was "sweeter when there were servants" but "when there was servants."

Doesn't that tell you something about that man? Doesn't that tell you that to this upper-middle-class Englishman, servants were not individuals? Isn't he saying that to him servants was a class? That second singular verb–*life was sweeter when there was servants*–tells us that to Daddy Nostalgia, they were not faces, *they* was a service.

I cannot imagine a do-it-yourself American erasing the individual and saying life was sweeter when there was servants. An American would say, "Life was sweeter when there were servants." And then he would quickly add that he paid his full share of the Social Security taxes for each of those individuals.

What was true for Oscar Wilde a hundred years ago is still true today. The differences between British English and American English reflect some of the differences between us, for language does reflect the culture of a nation.

–✦–

Consider some words that other nations have that we do not. The Italians, for example, have a word, *culaccino,* for the wet ring left by a wineglass on a table. Does that tell us something about what matters to the Italians?

The Germans, on the other hand, have a word, *schadenfreude,* that means taking delight in the misfortune of others. We may all do it, but in English we are not so proud of it as to have a word for it.

In Yiddish, the language that rose out of the ghettos and shtetls of eastern Europe, where families that prayed together stayed together, there arose a word that reflects their–dare I say?–life-style. The word is *machatonim. Machatonim* is the Yiddish word for the relationship between your parents and your spouse's parents. When I got married, my mother and my mother-in-law became related. They became *machatonim.* When your children marry, you acquire *machatonim.* Their in-laws are your *machatonim. Machatonim* is a cozy puppy of a word; it is a word that reflects the importance of the extended family in Jewish ghetto life. Isn't it wonderful to have a single word that expresses a complex relationship? *Machatonim.* I would like to give you that word today. But be careful. Be careful before you accept. Because if you accept this word, it is a lot like accepting the gift of a puppy. You will have to deal with it; your life will change. When you adopt a word from another culture, a word that reflects another culture, it begins to shape yours.

We adopted *croissant,* and our menus changed. We adopted *glasnost,* and our thinking about the Soviet Union changed. If you accept the gift of *machatonim,* you will have a degree of awareness that you have not had before. And that is because language certainly does reflect culture–not only of a nation but of an individual–but it also defines culture, and therein lies a responsibility. If you have a word for the parents of your child's in-laws, for the relationship between your parents and your parents-in-law you will think about them more. You may even think about them differently.

Our way of using language actually influences our view of the world. It shapes our thinking, and that shapes our culture. There are evenings when I sit in the bathtub feeling sorry for adjectives. In a few years, I think they will be whittled down to two: *fantastic* and *unbelievable* for adults and *neat* and *gross* for kids . . . unless, of course, you are discussing wine.

"Smooth, concentrated and well behaved," said a recent *New York Times* review of a California wine. Another connoisseur declared the same wine to have a "full luscious bouquet with an intense finish." Yet another found it "harsh and discordant on the palate with an astringent nose."

I feel sorry for the verbs *ruminate, saunter,* and *warble.* I believe that people in our society no longer ruminate or saunter or warble because we've forgotten the words for them. I sincerely feel that if we could resurrect the word *lullaby,* we would stand a good chance of hearing one on MTV.

—✛—

A few years ago, my local paper ran an article under the headline "Audiences Find Howie Mandel a Real Scream" (*Florida Times-Union;* July 21, 1986, syndicated article by Larry McShane). It begins like this:

> When words escape Howie Mandel, he screams—at the top of his lungs. "When I'm screaming, there's absolutely nothing else in my head," admits the off-the-wall comedian, whose new concert album . . . opens with a sequence of Howie howling. "People think the scream is funny, but I'm screaming because I'm standing in front of a lot of people with nothing to say."

Maybe Howie Mandel can act, but he can't talk. When he appears on talk shows, it becomes obvious that if a writer, someone who knows how to use language, has not given him something to say, there's absolutely nothing in his head. What if, instead of a scream, he had a few words in his head, then a random thought might form. And that thought just might be worth listening to. Just might be funny. Who does he think he is? Asking people to pay money for a record to hear a sequence of his screaming? Since when is a scream a substitute for wit?

People quote Woody Allen: "I am not afraid of death; I just don't want to be there when it happens."

People still quote Groucho Marx: "I wouldn't want to belong to any club that would accept me as a member."

Who will quote Howie Mandel? The expression is: you have to be there. Isn't his scream like the monkey salting potatoes, something he can communicate only to members of his audience? I hope that like the boy who yelled wolf, Howie will scream once too often, and people will simply stop listening.

Can you think about any concept if you don't have the word for it? Try to think about making brownies without words. Now, try to think about privacy or conformity or loyalty without thinking about the words for those concepts. If we have a word for something, our thoughts about it are clearer. Words define our thinking. And that's the truth.

—+—

When language gets sloppy, thinking gets sloppy.

Don't knock good sentence structure to me.

Don't tell me that Winston tastes good like a cigarette should. That commercial should have been banned for its bad effect on grammar long before it was banned for its bad effect on health. Can you see where it has taken us? *We do it like you'd do it when we do it like you'd do it at Burger King.* I passed a Village Inn on State Road 13 that had a huge banner proclaiming that they served Breakfast Like You Like It. Surely, this world would be a sadder and less magical place if William Shakespeare had taken us to Arden Forest in a play called *Like You Like It.*

In one of my books, *Up From Jericho Tel,* a character in the story by the name of Tallulah says, "Never have a long conversation with anyone who says 'between you and I.'" Another time Tallulah says, "Always use good grammar. It's like wearing designer clothing. People may not like your style, but they will pay attention to the cut of your cloth."

Listen to John Simon's review of *Miss Saigon* (*New York,* April 22, 1991):

Though the surface sound is vaguely with-it and tough, underneath is . . . the fake gentility of our composer's . . . comment about a news photo . . .

showing a child being snatched from a Vietnamese mother: "This photograph was, for Alain and I, the start of everything." That ghastly genteelism . . . "for Alain and I," tells it all: Miss Saigon is a show for people who say 'for you and I,' but not for me.

Let me give you another example of how language actually influences our view of the world.

There was once a boy who could not begin a sentence without repeating the initial sound or syllable in it. This boy had a wise father who told everyone in the household to listen to the child as if he spoke as normally as they did. Friends were asked to cooperate, and when the youngster started kindergarten, the father went to the teacher and asked that she do the same. The teacher replied that the school had a speech therapy program that would help a stutterer.

And the wise father said, "No, thank you. I don't want him put in therapy. I don't want him called a stutterer. If he has no word for it, he can't think of himself as one."

The teacher cooperated, and so did friends. Even relatives did. And the little boy said to me once when he was about ten years old, "You know, Mom, I used to have trouble saying some sounds. Like at the beginning of a sentence, I would go I-I-I-I-I. That was a funny kind of baby talk."

At a critical time, that son of mine did not have the word, the language tool, to identify himself as a stutterer, and so he never feared being one, and he is not one. Today he is a happy and successful man and the father of two of my five perfect grandchildren.

—+—

Think about how language shapes reality for the farmer. A farmer has a whole vocabulary of words for soil. In a single acre he can find combinations of silt, sand, clay, loam and gravel to which he assigns a whole poetry of names. Whereas he sees silt-loam as Kendaia and gravelly silt-loam as Honeoye, we see only dirt.

Don't tell me that everyone is entitled to "their" opinion, and don't tell me any athlete or rock star or TV star who says "you know" four times in a single sentence deserves to be listened to. Don't tell me that. Because when I hear such groping, sloppy speech, I know that it is the result of sloppy thinking, and furthermore, I know—and I can't make this point strongly enough—such sloppy speech causes sloppy thinking.

Language, then, is not only our link to a whole cultural past, it also shapes the way we see the present. But when one writes for children, one must also consider something else—the future. All writing for children is, in a sense, writing for the future.

A child is, in a sense, a stranger to even his own language. When an adult writes for children, she is writing as one who is living somewhere within the language pattern of culture, and she is writing for someone who is standing on its edge. So, as an adult writing for children, I must have my language reflect a culture, but I must also allow my language to be a tool that pokes holes in its hard outer edge. I want my books to let my readers move—saunter— a little bit deeper inside the pattern. I want them to be aware of other scenes, to ruminate on other thoughts, other kinds of soil.

Upon hearing a French song, my daughter, Laurie, once said to me, "Listening to a song in a foreign language is like looking at an abstract painting." She is right. Listening to a song in a foreign language is like looking at a painting where all the components—color, line, form—are familiar, but the pattern just doesn't make sense.

When I write for children, I don't want everything to be an abstract painting. I don't want everything to be unfamiliar, but I don't want everything to be familiar either. I want my readers to see reflections of things they know, but I want also to introduce them to something new. Let them find enough familiar symbols so that they will feel at home in my books, but also let them gather together the symbols of a different—or perhaps, broader—reality.

Let them read about the importance of having a secret inside like Claudia Kincaid in *From the Mixed-up Files of Mrs. Basil E. Frankweiler*. Let them read that being a liberated woman meant to Eleanor of Aquitaine very much what it means to Gloria Steinem—even though the trappings are different. Let them meet a human and uncertain Leonardo da Vinci. Let them read about what can show up when you are invisible, as Jeanmarie and Malcolm are in *Up From Jericho Tel*.

As a writer of books for children it is my responsibility to give them words so that they can have the thoughts. Could the Japanese think about truth if they didn't have a word for it? Can you keep any out-of-sight problem in mind if you don't have the symbols for it? For most of us those symbols are words. When the words form patterns, we have language.

I bring all of my adulthood to my writing for children. I make every effort to help children hear the language of my culture, a culture that reaches into the past and stretches over the present. Because language not only tells you the shape of a culture but also helps shape it, I make every effort to expand the perimeter of their language, to set a wider limit to it, to give them a vocabulary for alternatives, perhaps.

The politician's lethal weapon, the writer's principal tool, and Adam's gift are one and the same: *language*. Like a weapon, we must keep it accurate; like a tool, we must keep it in good working order; and like a gift, we must cherish it.

—✢—

Humpty Dumpty said to Alice:

> "When I use a word, it means just what I choose it to mean—neither more nor less."
> "The question is," said Alice, "whether you can make words mean so many different things?"
> "The question is," said Humpty Dumpty, "which is to be master—that's all."

Which is to be master, indeed. You or the word. Only a Humpty Dumpty can be master by proclamation. The rest of us are fated to learn the territory if we are to rule it. But once learned, we can shape it. We can shape it into something funny or something sad. We can make it show, and we can make it tell, and some of us, some of us who are very lucky, can shape language into books for children—and that is something that my IBM computer cannot do by word processing, and Humpty Dumpty cannot do by proclamation.

—✢—

To be able to stand here and talk about language and books and children has been a privilege and a pleasure. I can think of no better way to express my gratitude than by using a gutsy, straightforward, plain Old English word: Thanks.

# Into the 70s

The representation of blacks and other minorities in children's books arrived on the heels of the civil-rights movement of the sixties. At this time libraries were still the major market for children's books. In the mid-1960s the federal government passed legislation making money available for school libraries to stock their shelves. They needed books; tapes and computers were decades away. They needed a variety of books on a variety of subjects. Publishers scrambled to supply the demand. (Although submitted a year apart, my first and second novels both appeared in 1967. Publication of the first had been delayed because printers were catching up with publishers' orders of backlist titles.) This influx of money from the Great Society produced the first major surge in the number of children's books being published. The time had come not only for more books but also for books dealing with more subjects.

Every swelling in the body of permissible subject matter gave birth to a group ready to apply an ice pack. Every new allowable word gave birth to a set of word watchers waiting with Wite-Out.

Protest groups are as American as the Boston Tea Party. Only the agenda changes.

For example, *From the Mixed-Up Files of Mrs. Basil E. Frank-weiler,* which was published in the fall of 1967, has as its protagonist a twelve-year-old girl named Claudia who has run away from home. She has taken her brother Jamie with her. She tells him, "I, Claudia Kincaid, want to be different when I go back. Like being a heroine is different."

In the year of its publication, one reviewer objected to "a gratuitous reference to drugs in an otherwise pleasing story."

The gratuitous reference appears as follows:

[*Claudia and Jamie Kincaid are leaving the Donnell Library in New York, where they have done some research on the works of Michelangelo. Jamie spies a Hershey's almond bar, still in its wrapper, lying in a corner of the stair landing. He picks it up.*]

"You better not touch it," Claudia warned. "It's probably poisoned or filled with marijuana, so you'll eat it and become either dead or a dope addict."

Jamie was irritated. "Couldn't it just happen that someone dropped it?"

"I doubt that. Who would drop a whole candy bar and not know it? . . . Someone put it there on purpose. Someone who pushes dope. I read once that they feed dope in chocolates to little kids, and then the kids become dope addicts. Then these people sell them dope at very high prices which they just can't help but buy because when you're addicted you have to have your dope. High prices and all. And Jamie, we don't have that kind of money."

What would that reviewer think about this letter I received in the fall of 1993 from Robert G.?

. . . Nice story you wrote about Jamie and Claudia and their Runaway trip. It was the best story Ive heard from you El Konisburg . . . I liked when Claudia wants to be a heroine. Now I know that that means a girl hero. I thought That was only a drug. But Now I know that means a girl hero.

Would the reviewer, who in 1967 was offended by my brief reference to drugs, be equally offended by a young reader who in 1993 needs an explanation for *heroine* but not *heroin?* Or would that same reveiwer perhaps have a daughter or granddaughter who in 1993 is a member of the campus feminist group called Womyn of Antioch and is offended by Claudia's thinking of herself as a *heroine* instead of a *hero?* For every one of us who says *actress* or *hostess* or *priestess,* there is a word watcher, ready with Wite-Out and caret, who believes that, be they male or female, the correct words are *actor, host,* and *priest.*

There has always been something to offend someone, and there always will be.

If it's not one word, it's another. If it's not one subject, it's another. The subjects change, the words change, and so have the offended. Objections that were once the quirky comments of a single person have become agendas, and nowadays every agenda has behind it a group ready to mount a protest.

Throughout the years of my incumbency as a writer, protest groups have changed not only what they fight but how they fight. As soon as they reach a certain critical mass, they need an office, a staff, and a spokesperson. Spokespersons, too, have changed. Whereas they were once the leaders who rose from the grassroots organization, that is no longer the case. Nowadays, like it or not, spokespersons arise full-grown and go to the head of an interest group, not necessarily out of conviction. Like the knights of the middle ages, there are some who will defend whatever cause pays their way. They've become hired guns.

Take the case of Candy Lightner. In 1980, Ms. Lightner's thirteen-year-old daughter was killed by a drunk driver in a hit-and-run accident. She founded the organization MADD, Mothers Against Drunk Driving. By 1985 the organization had a national membership of thousands and a budget of more than $10 million. That year, Ms. Lightner, as their chief executive, requested a $10,000 bonus over the $76,000 she earned; however, earlier that year MADD was criticized for spending too much on fundraising and too little on programs, and Ms. Lightner was fired.

On January 15, 1994, the *New York Times* carried an article under the headline "Founder of Anti-Drunk-Driving Group Now Lobbies for Breweries."

> . . . after years of working for stiffer drunk-driving laws, Ms. Lightner is now lobbying against laws that would lower the standard blood-alcohol reading at which it becomes illegal to drive . . .

Ms. Lightner said that she saw nothing strange in her decision to join a lobbying group that represents the American Beverage Institute.

If one considers that a free lance needs a cause, one can agree with Ms. Lightner. The important principle is not the agenda; the important principle is that there be sides to an agenda. And in that way, these protest groups have become divisive. They must maintain divisiveness if they are to be paid to do away with it.

—✛—

In 1976, the year of our nation's bicentennial, the year *Painting a Novel for Children* was written, special interest groups were proliferating and drawing up new agendas.

# 3. Painting a Novel for Children

Among the battery of tests my husband gives to persons he assesses for hiring or promotion is a test called the TAT, the Thematic Apperception Test. This test consists of asking a person taking the test to write a story about each of a number of pictures. The pictures—sometimes of people, sometimes of landscapes—are all, to some degree, ambiguous. He also asks the person being evaluated to assign titles to their stories.

Over the years some of the people taking the test have asked David what he does with their stories when he is finished with them, and David's standard reply is: I give the good ones to my wife.

Well, he doesn't.

He doesn't ever let me read them. Not even the sexy ones.

And he won't tell me the titles. He says that my own titles have caused trouble enough already. Kids can neither pronounce nor spell them, and he can hardly remember them. David says that if I want to see the stories told from the TAT cards, I should take the test myself. He would administer it. I tell him no. I have told him no for all the years we have been married. I will continue to tell him no forever. I also refuse to take the Rorschach.

David tells the story about the man taking the Rorschach who interpreted each of the inkblots in a very libidinous

**40**

manner. When the tester said, "You seem, sir, to find a sexual connotation in everything," the man replied, "Well, it's your fault for showing me all those dirty pictures."

There is a lively connection between pictures and books. I don't mean picture books. I mean the connection between the art of painting a picture and the art of writing a book. There is a relationship between the way in which an artist uses his tools and the way in which a novelist uses his.

I would like to explore those parallels with you. I would like to make graphic the connection between a visible work of art–a painting–and a verbal work, a novel–most particularly, a novel for children.

—+—

Years ago, when I first started to write, I would go to work in the mornings as soon as my children left for school. When they came home for lunch, I would read them what I had written. Laurie, my daughter who was eight at the time, began a set of illustrations for the story I was writing and reading in installments, the story that became the novel *Jennifer, Hecate, Macbeth, William McKinley and Me, Elizabeth*. I saved those drawings, and I happen to have one right here.

This is our heroine, Elizabeth, finding a note on the Jennifer tree.

I was, of course, charmed by Laurie's effort. I told her that I liked her drawing very much. I did. I still do. But being the ex-teacher/ever-mother, I also told her that the sky should come all the way down to the ground.

She looked up at me and answered, "Nope. I've been there, and it doesn't."

Thus my young artist summarized with

the tools she was given the world as she knew it. And what were those tools—other than crayons and paper? They were line, color, and an idea. The idea was not her own; she was, after all, doing an illustration of someone else's thought, but with line and color she had made something personal of it. She had given someone else's idea a personal style. Style is not a basic tool, but it does lend a touch of class.

A writer of fiction uses the same basic tools as my daughter did. A writer of fiction uses line; we call it *plot*. But it is essentially the same thing: how do we get from here to there in our story? He uses color; we call it *characterization*. And he uses an idea; we call it *theme*. All of these materials—line, color, idea; plot, characterization, theme—serve to give form to the world as the writer/artist sees it.

An interesting phenomenon of this century has been the fragmentation of these tools both in the graphic arts and in fiction. Let me show you some fragments, some parallels between modern art and modern fiction.

Here is an artist, Henri Matisse, who has chosen to use only a single tool: line.

Do we still have a work of art?
I would say yes.

Just as in the Middle Ages astrolabes were both tools and works of art, so can this single tool, line, be a work of art.

But what don't we have? Obviously, we don't have shading, and we don't have depth. We have something that is often executed quickly and experienced quickly. We have, in effect, a quick read. We have, however, the right to bring to this line drawing whatever depths we choose. Layers of meaning can be added at our discretion and within our ability to do so. The artist has left us a lot of white space to fill in as we choose. In times past, such line drawings were considered preliminary to the final work, a sharpening of one's tools, so to speak.

Suppose a person chooses to write in the manner that this painting was done. Suppose a writer chooses to use line—story line or plot. What do we have? We have mysteries. We have thrillers. We have books that move swiftly from scene to scene, each one advancing the story line. We have books that skim and are skimmed. In their limited way, they, too, are works of art. They are often executed quickly, but they take enormous skill. And there is a place for these two-dimensional, line-drawing books. They fill a real need. Let me give you an example.

My husband and I were returning to the East Coast of the United States from Japan. As we were boarding the plane, I noticed a woman who had an Agatha Christie tucked inside her lightweight net carry-on. I had one tucked inside mine. I had *The ABC Murders* and she had *Nemesis.* I finished my Christie as well as *The Day of the Condor,* another line drawing. I am not a speed reader—it is a long flight—and I went searching for her. Holding out *The ABC Murders,* I asked, "Can we negotiate a trade?" "Oh, my dear," she said, "I fell asleep and haven't finished mine." Her husband looked up and said, "Would you consider trading an Agatha Christie for a Rex Stout?" I would. We traded. Thus, we both had a story line to get us from East to West.

One year I drove a car pool with a bunch of sixth-graders in the rear seat who spent the time from home to school and back again trading Hardy Boys and Nancy Drews. These straight-line plot books have charted the path for many travels for many ages and age levels.

Line-drawing books can decorate our minds just as line drawings can decorate our office walls. As suspenseful, as tension-producing as they may be, they represent escape from tension. There is never any worry for the reader about "getting the point." The story is the point. A person putting down an intricately plotted novel doesn't worry about whether or not he got the author's message. The medium is the message.

When a person writes for children, she must give them this part of her art. For decoration, of course, but also for the young readers' self-assurance. That way, the most timid and the most reluctant reader can put the book down and think: I got from there, the beginning, to here, the end. As a writer of children's books, I never underestimate the sense of satisfaction a child gets from having finished. A plotline is the best means of hanging a tale.

Sometimes a line drawing gets colored.

When that happens, we have *The Great Parade* by Fernand Léger.

What is a colored plotline? A story with a strong plot, but one that contains characters that have some dimension. When finished, a reader feels that she has enjoyed meeting the characters and has been more involved with what is happening to them as contrasted to what is happening. I think of the mysteries of Josephine Tey for this kind of reading, and of her works, *The Daughter of Time* comes first to mind.

What if we have only color and no line? We have then character sketches and mood pieces. We have, for example, that bright and jittery piece by J. D. Salinger called *Seymour: An Introduction.*

Look at this work called *Composition* by Wassily Kandinsky.

He has used color exclusively and loosely.

Close your eyes.

How much of this painting can you remember?

Where were the blues and where were the reds?

Compare your short-term memory of this painting with that of *The Great Parade*. *The Great Parade* certainly lacked depth, but the strong black lines helped to give the painting a focus and helped to stamp it in your memory.

When writing for adults, a person can use a single tool effectively and with style, but it has staying power only for sophisticated tastes. Children do not qualify. I think that writing pieces using only colors—even primary colors—is like painting a child into a corner that is papered with fiction from *The New Yorker*. Most children need a story as a towline to drag them—they often are dragged—from one splash of color to the next.

Here is an artist, Georges Braque, who is consumed with getting across an idea. That was the raison d'etre of the art form called Cubism, of which this picture, called *Fruit Dish and Cards,* is representative.

Braque, who along with Pablo Picasso invented Cubism, wanted to show objects, landscapes, and people as many-faceted solids, thus reducing all their subjects to a network of angles and planes.

Their influence on other artists was pervasive.

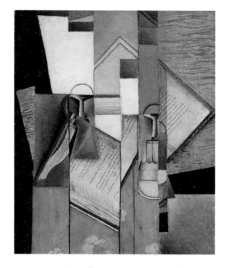

Look at Juan Gris's *The Book*

or Marcel Duchamp's *Bride* and

*The Passage from Virgin to Bride*

or Gris's *The Violin,*

and it is clear how much alike work that is in service to an idea begins to look.

As they refined their invention, Picasso and Braque deepened their collaboration. They began to treat the same subjects, and their pictures began to flatten.

So we have Picasso's *Violin and Guitar,* which is not very different from Braque's *Man with Guitar.* (The Picasso is smaller.)

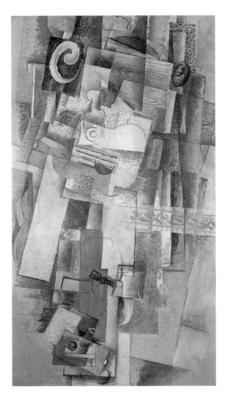

Or we have Braque's *Violin and Palette* or Picasso's *The Violin.* (The Picasso is smaller.)

As a last feature of Cubism, Picasso and Braque did away with the distraction of color, and their line became more and more fragmented.

## TalkTalk

The results were—left to right, top to bottom—*Ma Jolie (Woman with a Zither or Guitar)* by Picasso, *The Portuguese* by Braque, *Man with Clarinet* by Picasso, and *Woman with a Mandolin* by Braque.

Do the names of the artists matter? Without the signature, can you distinguish the Cubist paintings of Braque from those of Picasso? During the height of their collaboration, Picasso and Braque couldn't distinguish their own work.

When great artists become consumed with getting across an idea, their products become interchangeable.

Do the names of the paintings matter? Does the subject—be it man, woman, or zither—matter?

When great artists become consumed with getting across an idea, we get dry, flat, dun-colored works of art that look like worn linoleum. When all of an artist's tools are subordinated to an idea, he sacrifices his most personal gift: his style.

Whenever an idea is imposed upon works of art, giants become anonymous slaves. This happened to the pre-Raphaelites in 1848 in England. And it happened again when Joseph Stalin devised Socialist Realism in the Soviet Union in 1934. When Soviet artists were forced to paint a required theme, heroic idealization of work and workers, it became impossible to distinguish one socialist realist painter from another; they all looked like Norman Rockwell figures with thunder-thighs.

Conformity has a deadening effect on art. When all of an artist's tools become subservient to a single idea, his work becomes—as the Cubists' paintings did—deadly impersonal.

—✝—

Although there is great license in subject matter when writing for children today, there appears to be a tunneling of permissible philosophical position. And that bordering, that enclosing, is threatening the idea base that has been broadened in recent decades. Sex and pot have been allowed into the consecrated territory of children's literature, but there are forces afoot that deem certain ideas so important that all color, all line, all style must serve them.

There exists a publication called *Interracial Books for Children Bulletin* that considers it one of its responsibilities to reevaluate the classics, not in the broad sense of literary merit but in the limited sense of how these books treat race and sex.

In a box on page 6 of the volume 6, number 7, 1975, issue of *Interracial Books for Children Bulletin,* under a headline "Racist and Sexist Classics" the following appears:

> Many children's books about the revolutionary period that are regarded as classics are racist and sexist. Following are sample quotes from several such books.
>
> *Johnny Tremain* by Esther Forbes (Houghton Mifflin, 1943) winner of the Newbery Medal and considered a classic on the American revolution.

(And if I may add a personal note: one of the best Newbery Books ever. When I received the award, one of my first bursts of pride was that a book of mine would take its place on an honored shelf with *Johnny Tremain*.) But to continue with the information about *Johnny Tremain* that is in a box on page 6 of the *Interracial Books for Children Bulletin* (ellipses not mine):

> White is synonymous with beauty: "He was a fine-looking young man, with fresh skin and thick blond hair . . . clean, clear blue eyes." Black is sinister: ". . . black as imps from Hell and skinny, slippery-looking old black slave. . . wiry black fingers. . ." Of John Hancock's slave: "[Jehu] came mincing in . . . rolling his eyes . . . that dressed up doll of a black boy . . ." Sexism is also evident: Of Mrs. Lapham: "Slowly like a great sow pulling out of a wallow . . . her enormous bosom heaving . . ." And "Men went to war and women wept. All was as it should be."

I will not at this time refute the distortions to which this researcher has subjected Ms. Forbes's depiction of black and white. Ms. Forbes does describe ugly white as well as good black—a small example will follow—and two of the quotations about Jehu are presented out of order as well as out of context; I cannot find the third at all. Let me, for the sake of making the point I want to make about conformity to an idea destroying style, defend Ms. Forbes's so-called sexist writing.

The re-reviewer complains that Ms. Forbes has written, "Slowly, like a great sow pulling out of a wallow, her enormous bosom heaving," and that such writing is sexist. Let me put that quotation into context: Johnny Tremain has just spoken to Mr. Tweedie, the man whom Mrs. Lapham wants to be her business partner and whom she wants one of her daughters to marry. Johnny has come to realize that Mr.

Tweedie is a weakling and an opportunist. Mrs. Lapham is bending over repairing a smoking fire when Johnny tells her, "That squeak-pig is trying to horn in on breakfast." Then we have the famous quote.

> Slowly, like a great sow pulling out of a wallow, Mrs. Lapham got to her feet, glaring down at Johnny, her enormous bosom heaving.
> [Johnny says] "And I'm going to tell you what I think of that squeak-pig." Without a word and before he could finish his remarks or dodge, Mrs. Lapham gave him a resounding cuff on the ear.

If that is sexist, why isn't this non-sexist? and why is it not quoted?

> Lydia, the *handsome black* [italics mine] laundress at the Queen, extended his own eyes and ears into the very bedrooms of the officers, and often, as he helped her hang up sheets, she would tell him this and that . . .

Johnny, a boy, hanging up sheets and helping a black woman, a handsome black woman, to do so. Why doesn't the *Interracial Books for Children Bulletin* put this on the credit side of Ms. Forbes's ledger? But the more important question is this: Isn't Ms. Forbes to be allowed some personal style? Is not Mrs. Lapham's bosom, enormous though it may be, allowed to heave when she is angry? Is this gifted writer not to be allowed to use a metaphor about a sow immediately after Mr. Tweedie has been called a variety of pig? Is it permissible to call men pigs—male chauvinist or not—but not permissible to call women sows? Must a writer who can paint with words in Schiaparelli sow pink use a palette of only muted grays and browns?

About that other sexist remark: "Men went to war and woman wept." Madge, Mrs. Lapham's large daughter, has married a British soldier, one Sergeant Gale, a small man, one who is much smaller than she is.

> . . . Madge, even fatter since her marriage [was] seemingly more in love than ever with her little sergeant. Tears streamed down her thick, red cheeks . . . she flung herself upon Johnny.
> "I c-c-can't bear it. But he says he's g-g-got to go."
> Near-by tough little Sergeant Gale was strutting about like a bantam cock, roaring at one of his men whose buttons did not shine. He was pretending not to know that his wife was so near-by. He was really showing off in front of her and approved her presence. Men went to war and women wept. All was as it should be.

After reading this excerpt in context, is there any doubt at all that Ms. Forbes, with all the grace and wisdom of her talent, is having a Tory sexist, *a character in a novel,* express a sexist thought? Is there any doubt that Ms. Forbes is using one of the tools of the novelist's trade—colorful characters—to help tell her story?

Must we be totally colorless when describing sex and paint with Day-Glo red everything that has to do with the sex act?

In a piece entitled "Dirty Words," in the *New York Times Book Review* of August 8, 1976, Mr. Anthony Burgess makes a wonderful point.

> In 1960, I published a novel that had the sentence: "He looked him up and down from his niggerbrown shoes to his spinsterishly tightset lips and then said quietly: "_____off." In the new edition of 1975, the shoes and the lips are more generally and less offensively characterized, and the dirty word is set out in full. One semantic area has been freed from taboo; two others have been freshly enslaved by it. There is a lesson here: Human history does not depict the progressive throwing off of chains, merely

the exchange of one set of chains for another, or two others.

I do not know what librarians do these days with Conrad's "The Nigger of the Narcissus . . ."

I don't know either, but I do know what they do with *Huckleberry Finn* in New Trier, Illinois. They take him off the list, the required-reading list. The English Department there has removed *Huckleberry Finn* from the required-reading list. The parents of New Trier East High maintained that "the book's repeated references to 'niggers' were 'morally insensitive' and degrading and destructive to black humanity."

If I were one of the fifty blacks out of a school population of 6,387 students, I think I would feel patronized by having *Huckleberry Finn* removed from the library shelves to protect me. I think I would also feel cheated, cheated of a wonderful black hero named Nigger Jim, cheated of a wonderful treatment of one of the great moral dilemmas of my American history, cheated of a great seminal novel of my American literary heritage.

—✛—

June Jordan, black professor and poet, a woman whose work has been nominated for a National Book Award, was a guest on Mr. William Buckley's program, "Firing Line," in 1976. The subject was: Should books such as *Little Black Sambo* be on library shelves? I sent for a transcript.

> Mr. Buckley: . . . What you have is a bunch of text-books in which are located certain symbols of oppression, symbols of discrimination, which are nowadays perceived as being vicious, which were previously perceived as being purely

conventional—*Little Black Sambo* would be an obvious
example . . . Would you say that any school that
used it as part of the juvenile literature ought
not to qualify for the receipt of federal
funds?

Ms. Jordan: No, I would not. It would depend
altogether on how the book was used in the
schools.

Are the people of New Trier East High School saying
that *Huckleberry Finn* cannot be properly taught? As Oscar
Hammerstein said, "You have to be taught to be afraid
of people whose eyes are oddly made," and you have to
be properly taught to see that *nigger* is as outmoded a
name as *Huckleberry*. And so, too, is the thought, *nigger*. If
properly taught, the chapter called "The Rattlesnake
Skin" can do it all. This is the section where Huck
deceives the bounty hunters by cleverly making them believe
that he wants their help because no one else will give
it because "Pap has this fever." He cleverly leads them
to think that he is harboring some victims of smallpox
instead of a runaway slave. The bounty hunters sail away
leaving two twenty-dollar gold pieces to salve their con-
sciences.

Smallpox is a dinosaur of a disease. And *nigger* is a dinosaur
of a word, of a thought. But suppressing books that tell about
them will not alter the past.

—✛—

I want all the books on the shelves.

I want the books with dinosaur words like *nigger* that show
the skeletons in our national closet. I want books with the
word cunt as well as the word kike. Words don't scare me.
Suppressing them does.

Take away color; subdue every word to someone's idea of what is correct, and we will have the literary equivalent of *The Aficionado* by Picasso that looks a lot like Georges Braque's *Le Guéridon* that resembles Picasso's *Landscape at Céret.*

We will be left with works that have no color and no personal style. We will be left with works that are tight and controlled and dull. Very dull. Very, very dull.

Don't let current political correctness make Dick and Jane of children's literature.

—✜—

When writing for children, one must use all the tools at one's command: color, line idea.

Here is a painting that has all of these elements. It is Marc Chagall's *Self-Portrait with Seven Fingers.*

This is a work that is strongly and fully colored. Replete with distorted but recognizable objects, its elements are unified by the themes of identity and memory. The color and the characters are strong, and the story is told as much by symbol as by narrative. The Eiffel Tower tells us of the artist's Paris home, and the Hebrew writing in back of him, just over his head, tells us of his Jewish past. Everything is here, but it is not presented in a totally logical order. In short, we have here the heated, steamy world of William Faulkner. We have here a man who has sharpened his tools. He colors his characters distinctively—think of Temple Drake or the Snopeses—and he distorts reality enough to make us believe it. It is a work rich in metaphor and wit. The title, *Self-Portrait with Seven Fingers,* is appropriate, too. How often an artist must feel that he has seven fingers. And how often he must feel that five of the seven are thumbs.

What is the difference between that work of Chagall and this work?

Here again we have all the elements of a work of fiction: plot, characterization, and theme. But when we move from Chagall's work to this one, we move from fiction for adults to fiction for children. Here we have a straightforward telling. Here we have everything in its place; only proportion and perspective are distorted.

The painting is called *The Muse Inspiring the Poet.* The painter, Henri Rousseau, is called a primitive.

He was a Sunday painter. During the week, he worked as a customs officer, a douanier. (Lionel Trilling once said that the best children's books are written by people who have something else to do.)

Until a few years ago, primitive art was outside the body of work taken seriously by the critics. It spoke directly to the people. Until a few years ago, children's literature was outside the body of literature taken seriously by the critics. It, too, spoke directly to its people—young readers.

Another way in which this painting represents children's literature is that it exists outside the realm of good or bad taste. A person leads with his heart when deciding whether or not he loves that broad-faced muse in a lavender dress. A child reading a book leads with his heart, too. And there is something else that this painting shares with a work of children's fiction: freshness. I think every children's book should have that as well as color and line and underlying theme.

This artist has not skimped. He has used everything at his command: line, color, idea; plot, character, theme. Everything is represented in a straightforward, sincere manner—with wonderful and unexpected distortions for emphasis.

I see something else in this painting that a good work of fiction for children should have: a few elements of the landscape are unfamiliar. The unfamiliar elements are rooted in a very familiar looking lawn. I think a writer of children's books should also create this mix and match. Let the territory be familiar enough so that the reader is comfortable; make the landscape understandable. Introduce him to all the colors—white and yellow and red; brown and black. All the colors should be there. Use quality paint and brushes—good English—but vary the strokes. Some short, some long, some thin, some thick. Yes, some strokes have to be laid on thick. How can a person recognize purple prose if he has never seen it?

For all his childlike rendering, Rousseau has not skimped on his vocabulary of naive greens and sophisticated lavenders.

This particular painting has two other elements that make it an apt recital of what children's books should be. These two elements are not for every book, but they are often appropriate. One, the douanier, Rousseau, has painted no very great difference between the sexes. Dress for one, pants for the other, but they are more alike than they are different. Two, he has taken an abstract notion, inspiration, and made of it a concrete, very concrete, muse. Medieval artists did this all the time: the holy spirit was a dove, the light of God was a halo of whitish color, and the mouth of Hell was a voracious maw. Making the abstract concrete is not appropriate for every children's book, but done with panache, it adds wonder to the mix.

This painting has everything a children's novel should have: a plotline for those readers who need a rope—most of them do—to get from chapter to chapter. Characters to keep the chapters colorful and lively. And a theme for those readers who like to get more than is visible to the naked eye.

What else does a children's novel need? Paragraphs in all sizes from mountain to molehill. Some express sentences and some that whistle-stop. And words, words, words in every color from male-chauvinist-pink to black-is-beautiful.

Add one ingredient to that mix. Add a muse. The douanier, Rousseau, shows the muse reaching toward Heaven with one hand and touching the poet's shoulder with the other. I think he got it right. A muse touches the poet and makes everything work right. Poets call it a muse; critics call it inspiration. My readers call it magic. They, too, got it right.

# The 70s (continued)

Because children themselves often do not have the means to control what they read, their books of every genre from textbook to trade book must pass through more monitors—evaluators—than books for adults. In addition to the usual filters of publisher, editor, and critic, children's books pass through a net of parents, teachers, and librarians.

It is in the green room before the book gets to the parent/teacher/librarian stage that the critic waits. He prepares a book for blessing or banning.

In the world of adult publishing this is often the final stop. Sometimes, as in the case of *The Bridges of Madison County,* they dance right onto the boards with almost no critical reviews. Sometimes, as in the case of *Gone with the Wind,* they continue to perform successfully despite never having been taken seriously by the literary establishment.

For a long time, children's books were reviewed by user-friendly people, people who had contact with children. Reviewers acted as book counselors. They were not professional critics but teachers or librarians who arranged marriages between readers and books. They were not interested in demonstrating how literary or how avant-garde their reviews were. They knew literature and they knew children, and they were interested in making the relationship between the two work.

Before they attracted celebrity authors, children's books attracted celebrity reviewers. In 1972 the award panel for the National Book Award for Children's Literature drew two of three judges from their ranks. The award, initiated in 1969, was to be given to a juvenile book that a panel of judges considered the most distinguished, written by an American and published in the United States during the previous year. The award was discontinued in 1979.

In 1972 the National Book Award for Children's Literature went to Donald Barthelme for *The Slightly Irregular Fire Engine or The Hithering Thithering Djinn,* his only children's book. That year the jury failed to reach a unanimous agreement. Whereas the two celebrity jurors felt "that this is a book of originality, wit, and intellectual adventure," the third juror knew that whatever it was, it wasn't for children and made an unprecedented public statement that he had not concurred with the decision of the other two panelists. The third juror was Paul Heins, editor of *The Horn Book,* a bimonthly periodical devoted exclusively to children's literature.

The first printing of *The Slightly Irregular Fire Engine* was remaindered, a remarkably short shelf life for an award-winning children's book. Mr. Heins knew that children—not critics, not committees—are the sine qua non of children's books.

So much in our culture is new to children, there are so many firsts in their young lives, that they live on the cutting edge. They have little need for the avant-garde. The old-fashioned is new to anyone meeting it for the first time. And children—unlike critics, unlike committees—have only one agenda: intelligent enjoyment of the printed word. They are far less docile than adults when it comes to paying attention to professional critics. They do not hesitate to put back on its shelf a book that does not reach out to them. Affection for a book is its best award, and books that earn that award arrive from the hearts and minds of writers, not juries.

Real books, keeper books, take children someplace. They take them out of themselves or to a place deep inside themselves with a new sense of discovery.

"Going Home" grew out of my reflecting upon what books have meant to me as a reader and as a writer. It illustrates my belief that real books start in the hearts and minds of writers and, if the writer is lucky, real books find a home in the hearts and heads of children.

# 4. Going Home

Some years ago on a return trip from driving our daughter back to college in upstate New York, my husband and I decided to spend a few days in New York City. We checked into the Hilton Hotel at Rockefeller Center, prepared to spend our time going to foreign films and Broadway shows and visiting museums.

Both of us love to walk in the city, and we always chose to walk back to our hotel following our evening's entertainment. Each night we noticed some attractive and startlingly dressed ladies waiting at various spots along the Fifty-third Street side of the hotel. There was a convention of sociologists headquartered there at the time.

David and I were pretty sure that these women were not volunteering their services for any longitudinal study of patterns of culture in a modern urban center. We were pretty sure that the services they offered were of a more horizontal nature, and we felt that whatever they had to offer, it was not being volunteered.

They were there every night, beautifully made up, dressed not stylishly but with panache. They had a basic attention-getting style—something of a combination of Dolly Parton and Frederick's of Hollywood. David and I came to recognize a few of them and would nod hello to them as we came and went from the hotel.

We had theater tickets for our last evening there. As often happens, going to the theater in a taxi, the cross-town traffic was impossible. We realized that if we were not to miss the curtain, we would have to get out on Broadway and walk. We asked the driver to let us out at the next red light, and he did. We emerged into the Broadway throng and started pushing our way toward Forty-fifth Street. It happened—as it often does in a crowd as bustling as that one—that David and I got separated. He waited for me on the corner of Forty-fifth, and in the short time that it took for me to catch up with him, he was approached by a cheaply dressed and not altogether clean lady of the night.

I caught up with him in record time and took his arm in a proprietary manner and pulled him around the corner.

"You know," I said, "ours are much prettier."

By *ours,* of course, I meant the ladies outside the Hilton.

And why were they suddenly *ours?* Because in the short time that we had been there, the Hilton Hotel had become home. And a person has special feelings about home and about the people from home.

And more than that, I think that a person has a need for home.

And for going home.

And that is what I would like to talk about today. About going home.

There are many kinds of homes. There is the single-parent home, and there is the orphan home and the old-folks home and the foster home and the dormitory and the apartment and the condominium and—temporarily—the Hilton. But I will leave those kinds of homes—plus *a house is not a home*—to that convention of sociologists at the Hilton. There are other kinds of homes I would like to talk about today: homes that have relevance to the world of books, and most especially, children's books.

—✛—

The first kind of home I would like to talk about is the kind of home I reach for as a writer.

When someone writes a novel—especially a novel for children—he is going home in the sense that a home is where something is discovered or founded. Like Cooperstown, New York, is the home of baseball because that is where baseball was founded, and the University of Florida is the home of Gatorade because that is where Gatorade was invented. And Florence, Italy, is the home of the Italian Renaissance because Florence is where the Renaissance started in Italy.

Home for a writer is going home to where things were started. It is the place where there exists the protocell of emotions, the place where there exists the protomorphic ego, and the act of writing is the process of going home to where things got started. And that place is childhood.

When a person writes he returns home—to childhood—and in that sense, home is a time as well as a place. It is often a small, dark place where we were often frightened. Childhood as home was not always comfortable, and it is often not fun to return to, but it is a place we all carry around inside of us, and it must be looked into and occasionally aired out. It is the place where we felt both most belonging and, strangely, most singular. It is the place where we were most raw, most unvarnished, most uncluttered with the packaging of civilization. And this is what a writer returns to.

The first time I went home as a writer was in *Jennifer, Hecate, Macbeth, William McKinley and Me, Elizabeth*. I went back to the child in me who was the outsider. I returned to being the new kid on the block, to the place where I discovered loneliness and the need for a friend, just one, please God, instead of curly hair. That was in Youngstown, Ohio, where I attended William McKinley Elementary School for one half of fifth grade and all of sixth. I went home as Elizabeth and to the Elizabeth who still lives within me. I also went home as Jennifer, the friend that Elizabeth finds. In that case I returned to the place where I discovered other people's consciousness of my being a member of a minority group. I went back to the place where I discovered how much more satisfying it was to offer myself up for friendship, not as a plain old minority-group member but as something exotic, just to make myself more interesting, to make myself, I thought, more worthy of friendship.

I might add that this trip home was triggered by watching my own three children adjust to being the new kids on their block; their block was an apartment house in suburban New York.

When I went home in *About the B'nai Bagels,* I went to find the place in me where I discovered the joys of being a team player plus that other need, a room of one's own, the need to be private. I have said that this kind of going home means journeying to a place and time where discoveries are made, and this ride was not as long as some of the others have been. This time I had to go only as far as my freshman year at college. This time I returned to the place where I had left home and had moved into a dormitory and discovered that I wanted to be part of the group, this great gaggle of girls—there were no coed dorms back then—but that there was also a part of me that didn't want to belong. I was a slow developer in this respect because before leaving home, I did not know that such choices existed. My own three children made this discovery at a much younger age—at the age of Mark Setzer, the hero of *About the B'nai Bagels.*

In *(George)* I returned to the time—the critical time—when I thought I was losing contact with my inner self. It was a time even before I knew the words id or persona. It was a time when no one searched for an identity or spoke of an identity crisis. I knew only that I had this funny little woman who lived inside me: she was much older than I was, and although she didn't know the words for everything, she knew much more than I did. It was a time when my friends were screaming for attention, and so was she. I didn't want to lose my friends or lose touch with this funny old lady because she was a source of much amusement and nourishment and—even though I did not then know the word for it—*perspective* in my life.

I always try to go home, to childhood as it represents origins, when I write. Not only because I write for children but also because there is something honest and authentic about one's childhood. And honesty and authenticity are good places to start when writing anything.

When a person is middle-aged, there are many things that get in the way of going home.

There is, first of all, the discovery—the minute you sit down to write—that you have four inch-long whiskers growing out of your chin. It takes a trip to the mirror to examine them. That necessitates a trip to the medicine cabinet for the tweezers and then back to the mirror to pluck them. Then back to your desk to think about those four hairs on your chin, to think that you don't remember having had a problem with chin hairs when you were a child. There were never any problems as definite and as numerical as chin hairs when you were a child. There were vague problems. There were fears and loose uncertainties. You rub your chin again, thinking (and incidentally checking for more hairs) and wondering about how to make concrete words out of those vague, pervading anxieties that existed at a time when you never had hairs appear full grown and an inch long out of your chin.

Chin hairs are one problem for a writer trying to go home.

There are other problems, too.

There are the inhibitions that have formed a scum over those protofeelings. There are the years and the events between the then and the now that have hardened into a scab. In its way, a scab is protective, and it is painful to lift that protective, ugly covering and examine the wound underneath.

But suppose a writer admits that the pain of not looking is worse than the pain of looking. Then there is the worry that even though you got home last time, you'll probably get lost this time, and there is the foregone knowledge that home is often cheaper and smaller and less attractively populated than we remembered it.

There is always the temptation to call off the trip.

But something drives us home. Something drives all of us there.

Because of what home is.

Home is "Something you somehow haven't to deserve" (Robert Frost). "The place we come from" (Herman Hesse). "The place they know how you feel about a banana" (Damon Runyon).

Home is, ultimately, the place where the truth, the awful truth, the naked truth, the *hairless* truth about ourselves, exists.

It is our genesis.

And that is what going home is about for a writer.

—✦—

There are also ways of going home as a reader. There are two ways that I would like to talk about. One is a certain kind of book that prepares your imagination for feeling at home away from home.

Perhaps, by contrasting two trips that my husband and I have taken, I can demonstrate this kind of going-home book.

Many summers ago we went to South America. We started our tour in Bogotá, Colombia. There, at the beginning, I felt that something was missing. I didn't know what. I thought about it for a time and then tried to pin it down by contrasting this with other trips we had taken. And that gave me a clue.

When we arrived in London, for example, the first thing we did was go to see the changing of the guard at Buckingham Palace. Even as I say this now, I am hearing in my head, "They're changing the guard at Buckingham Palace—Christopher Robin went down with Alice." Before ever getting to Buckingham Palace, I lived for a long time—a long, long time—with the changing of the guard there. *We saw a guard in a sentry box.* "'One of the sergeants looks after their socks,' said Alice." What fun it was to compare what I thought changing the guards would be like with what it actually was. Had Christopher Robin never gone down with Alice, I would have been robbed of half the pleasure of that very first morning in London because the whole thing could not have happened in my imagination before I saw it happening on the streets.

As a reader, I look for this kind of going-home book. I love books that give us place names, books that make a reality for us before we discover it. A reality more true than any travel guide can create because the geography of fiction is *peopled,* whereas that of travel guides is merely *placed.*

Place names exist all over England. A person gets a feeling of *déjà vu* wherever he turns. Can anyone visit Dorset and not in some sense feel that he, too, is one of Thomas Hardy's natives returning on a

> . . . Saturday afternoon in November . . . approaching the time of twilight, [as] the vast tract of unenclosed wild known as Egdon Heath embrowned itself moment by moment . . .

Can you drive through that country and not look for Eustacia Vye and Diggory Venn, the ruddleman, and Michael Henchard, the Mayor of Casterbridge?

Can anyone go to Canterbury–even in a Hertz–without also going "[E]asily on an ambling horse" with the Wife of Bath? Can anyone go to Yorkshire and not feel the ghosts of Heathcliff and Cathy on the moor?

The British have given us all these books, all these families, all these homes to go to. They have made us rich in adopted families. Thanks to a glorious body of literature, there is almost nowhere a person can go in England and not feel at home.

Allow me to contrast my first visit to England with my first trip to South America. In those days before the flowering of magical realism, I knew no centuries-old ghosts to travel with. There was one recent one.

There was *One Hundred Years of Solitude* by Gabriel Gárcia Márquez. He is Colombian. Let me read you a short paragraph from an interview with him that appeared on July 16, 1978 in the *New York Times Book Review.*

> Do you know that nowadays hundreds of people are visiting Aracataca, Colombia, which is the setting of *One Hundred Years of Solitude?* All sorts of people, including American scholars, come because they want to see the actual house, the actual tree and so forth mentioned in the novel. Now the local children, who know nothing about the book but who are eager to cash in on it, run up to the visitors and say, "For five centavos I'll show you the house," and then they lead the tourist off to any old house or any old tree and pretend it's the one from the novel.

Colombia has over four hundred thousand square miles, and England has fifty thousand. There is only one literary home in all of Colombia and that one is an agreed-upon myth, but in England, a person can hardly turn a corner without meeting someone from the literary home within us.

For that first trip to South America I missed bumping into people I'd met in the pages of a book. I missed having read books that would have given me a home away from home, books that would have prepared my imagination as it was prepared to go to Paris and find in the district that lies between the Latin Quarter and the Faubourg Saint-Marcel a certain lodging house

> owned by Madame Vauquer. It stands at the lower end of the Rue Neuve-Sainte-Geneviève, at the place where the street makes a sharp drop toward the Rue de l'Arbalète . . . [T]hese streets huddled between the domes of the Val-de-Grâce and the Panthéon . . .

Until I read *Père Goriot,* I didn't know that Paris as well as Rome has a Pantheon. I went to see it. But not only it. I went to see the descendants of Eugène Rastignac and Madame Vauquer.

I have never been to Russia, but I know that when I go—if ever I do—I shall visit St. Petersburg, and part of me will not be there at all but will be in another century, and I shall travel with Anna Karenina and Vronsky (even though I do not like them very much), and I shall look over a bridge at the Neva River, and Raskolnikoff will be breathing over my shoulder.

We don't like to walk alone.

Look at what happened to Vlad the Impaler. He was a Knight of the Dragon in the fifteenth century, a rather obscure knight, and then, at the end of the nineteenth century a rather obscure writer wrote a gothic novel about him and his castle. The writer was Bram Stoker, and the novel was *Dracula.* Look at what has happened since. The Romanian government has done to his castle in Transylvania what the children of Aracataca, Colombia, have done. They will show you the house, the castle, the staircase, the window, or anything else that Bram Stoker dreamed up.

I have never been able to get through James Joyce's *Ulysses,* yet I found myself thrilled to read in the travel section of a Sunday issue of my local paper:

> . . . Every June 16, Bloomsday, [Joyce's] faithful fans from all over the world don Edwardian dress and retrace street by street Leopold Bloom's odyssey about the city on that June Thursday in 1904. Along the way there are readings from the novel, restaurants offering "Bloom's menue," even a James Joyce look-alike contest.
>
> Dublin, says John Kidd, director of the James Joyce Research Center at Boston University, "has become a James Joyce theme park."

How hungry we are to walk with book people.

Doing so adds a dimension to reality.

A writer of books for children heightens reality for readers when he gives them place names to dream about. I know that Dickens and Mark Twain did that for me. And so did Kipling. And I am positively thrilled when I get letters from kids who tell me that they have visited the Metropolitan Museum of Art in New York City and to them it is not only the home of Rembrandt, Renoir, and Raphael but also the home of Claudia and Jamie Kincaid.

There are these books that I need as a reader—the books that create a reality before we discover it for ourselves. But there is a second kind of going-home book that I love just as much, and that is the kind that makes us discover a reality that we already know.

This is a breed of book that is *home* in the sense that we say an arrow hits home. We say, after closing the covers of this special kind of book, "That book, that chapter, that character sure struck home." These are the books that have passages that you have underlined before you send a paperback copy to your sister in Ohio.

Passages in this kind of book also evoke some place you've been, not a geographical location but an emotional state, or someone you've met—most often yourself. These on-target, at-home books produce that welcome shock of recognition.

Home can be a small place.

Once it was a guest editorial in *Newsweek* magazine in which Cyra McFadden described her reactions during a three-hour class in CPR, cardiopulmonary resuscitation. I smiled as I read, thinking: So did I. Oh! I thought as I read: Yes, yes, how embarrassing that had been. Then I clipped the article and routed it to the other members, the alumni, of my CPR class. It was marvelous. We all ended up feeling a sort of conspiratorial communion with Ms. McFadden, and seeing our reactions in print gave our experiences in the CPR training class a heightened sense of importance and reality.

We returned to our feelings in the classroom. We returned to our alma mater. To home.

What that on-target, hitting-home article did for me and the other members of my CPR class—giving us a heightened sense of importance and reality—certain books do in a deeper and more personal way. These are the books that reflect us, that distill our lives into paragraphs and give us essence. They are not the same for everyone because, obviously, we do not all come from the same place. Some great, universal books are apartment houses where there is a room for everyone. Some great books like *Anna Karenina* or *The Red and the Black* are so big that they have at least a room or two in them where anyone can feel at home.

Others are small, detached dwelling places where we enter and immediately recognize everything and everyone described therein. Reading *Mrs. Beneker* by Violet Weingarten was this kind of going home for me. It is the story of a middle-class, middle-aged suburban woman with grown children, who is slightly baffled but never defeated by the life she leads. This book was going home for me in the same way as reading *The Happy Hooker* would–I imagine–be going home for certain ladies to whom a house is not a home.

Years ago, *The Catcher in the Rye* was a going-home book for me. Later, it was for my older son, my daughter, my younger son as each of them read it. And five years ago, when I reread it and met again and was charmed again and laughed again at Holden Caulfield, it was once again a going-home book.

And before *The Catcher in the Rye* there was *Junior Miss* by Sally Benson.

And before *Junior Miss* there was *Little Women*.

And before that there was nothing.

Nothing and nothing and nothing.

As I was growing up, I never found the kind of going-home book where I could recognize the heroine as me. I could identify with lots of heroines–with *The Little Princess,* say, or with *Mary Poppins*–but I never enjoyed the shock of recognition that going-home books afford. And I missed them. And just imagine all the African-American children and all the Mexican-American children who missed them for a long, long time after I did.

Now I thank goodness that there were no going-home books for me when I was a child. Because I worried that my own three children would miss them as they started growing up, and I began to write so that they would have a book that was on target for them, a book that would reflect their kind of growing up as books had not reflected mine.

–✦–

What kept me from finding myself in books as I was a little girl growing up in small towns in Pennsylvania? Why would it happen that when I picked up a book that promised me that I would meet typical children in a typical small town, I would read about someone named Betsy who took naps, for God's sake, and who had a patient mother and a maid. I lived in small towns where the mothers hired out as maids, not where they hired them.

Were books that happened to be a true reflection of life in a small town, the touching books, the on-target, the going-home books, just not being written, as my children say, "back then"?

Maybe they weren't.

Maybe.

But I don't think so.

I think that there were writers who were going home, but I think there were, *back then,* editors who didn't like to think that home could include quarrels among siblings and cross mothers and bathrooms.

These editors are a dying breed. Dying but not dead. They live! They live, not in the trade book divisions of publishing houses, but in the textbook divisions. Of certain publishing houses. And they exist because they still don't want to face the fact that we all go to the bathroom, and we don't take doing so very seriously.

They do, though.

I would like to share with you a three-way correspondence concerning me, my editor, and some editors of a certain textbook publishing house. It begins with this letter to me from my editor, Jean Karl.

Dear Elaine:

We have had a request to adapt material from THE MIXED-UP FILES . . . for a textbook. I am enclosing the material that came from the publisher. Do look it over and see what you think. If you don't like it at all and don't approve of what they are doing, just say so and I will tell them.

Best wishes, etc. . . . Jean Karl

The letter she enclosed was as follows:

Dear Mrs. Konigsburg:

I am writing in the hope that you will allow us to use an excerpt from FROM THE MIXED-UP FILES OF MRS. BASIL E. FRANKWEILER in the revision of our sixth grade reader. There are two reasons why I am very anxious to use this particular piece. First it is a representative selection of a delightful book that I want to share with our readers. Secondly, I am planning to follow your story with a photo essay/article on a very exciting Children's Museum in Connecticut. It is my hope that the two pieces taught together will give children a new, more positive approach to museums, both traditional and experimental. I hope they will be inspired to explore museums and your other works with equal fervor.

Due to space considerations, I have been forced to cut several passages from Chapter Three. Your suggestions and criticisms on the editing would be greatly appreciated.

Very sincerely . . . etc. . .<br>Editor, Reading Basics

Chapter 3 of *From the Mixed-up Files of Mrs. Basil E. Frankweiler* deals with Claudia Kincaid and her brother Jamie who in running away from home have arrived in New York City. They have come to the Metropolitan Museum of Art, where they intend to live in comfort and a bit of luxury. They take a map from the information stand, and Claudia selects where they will hide during that dangerous time immediately after the museum is closed to the public and before all the guards leave. She decides that she will go to the ladies' room and Jamie will go to the men's room. She instructs Jamie to go to the one near the restaurant on the main floor. Thereupon, they have a brother-sister discussion.

Jamie: "I'm not spending a night in a men's room. All that tile. It's cold. And, besides, men's rooms make noises sound louder."

Claudia explains to Jamie that he is to enter a booth in the men's room, "And then stand on it."

"Stand on it? Stand on what?" Jamie demands.

"You know," Claudia insists. "Stand on it!"

"You mean, stand on the toilet?" (Jamie needed everything spelled out.)

"Well, what else would I mean? What else is there in a booth in the men's room? And keep your head down and keep the door to the booth very slightly open," Claudia says.

Jamie: "Feet up. Head down. Door open. Why?"

Claudia: "Because I'm certain that when they check the ladies' room and the men's room, they peek under the door and check only to see if there are feet. We must stay there until we're sure all the people and guards have gone home."

That passage is part of chapter 3, and chapter 3 is what the publisher wanted to use for its new sixth-grade reader. I looked over the materials they had sent via my editor and sent the following letter:

Dear Jean:

Enclosed are the materials from the textbook publisher. I think it will be fine for them to use part of my book FROM THE MIXED-UP FILES . . . if they use the material as I have edited it per the request in their letter. I have cut out as much as they have in the interest of space without destroying the characterizations of the two children and without leaving information dangling in the manner they did on pages 3 and 6 of their copy. If they should decide that the material needs further editing, I would like to see it before it goes into print.

Sincerely . . . etc.

# E.L. Konigsburg

Next in this saga comes a letter from my editor at Atheneum.

Dear Elaine:
I am enclosing material included in the letter that came from the [textbook] publisher today. I think this is ridiculous. I would say to them to "Go fly a kite." Do let me know what you think.
Sincerely . . . etc. Jean Karl

The letter she wanted to tell them to go fly a kite about is as follows:

Dear Miss Karl:
I'm so sorry to trouble you again—I'd hoped we were through with FROM THE MIXED-UP FILES OF MRS. BASIL E. FRANKWEILER. But alas, standing on the toilets just didn't make it through editorial conference last week.
Would Elaine Konigsburg be kind enough to take a look at our deletion? Manuscript page attached.
With thanks . . . etc. Rights and Permissions, Department of Reading Basics.

I reread the standing-on-toilets section that I've just presented, and I didn't think it was so very bad, so I wrote the following letter directly to the rights and permissions editor of the Department of Reading Basics.

Dear Mrs.[Editor]:
During the past year I have appeared on several different talk shows, some TV, some radio—local productions in various parts of the country: the South, the Midwest, the West. Last spring I was interviewed on one of New York City's public radio stations. Something happened at that session that I would like to share with you.
My editor and I arrived early, even before the interviewer got there. The lady who produces the show met us in the studio where the interview was

to take place. She was a native New Yorker; she knew that I had arrived from Jacksonville, Florida. She explained to me that the interviewer would concentrate on questions about my newest book and would in no way embarrass me by asking personal questions such as how many times I was married and/or divorced. I realized that she was trying to put me at ease; she couldn't know that it has been a long time since I have experienced any nervousness about public appearances . . . I listened to her politely and smiled a great deal. I have very large front teeth, and sometimes my smile appears overabundant and anxious. The producer then attempted to reassure me further by telling me that the interview would be *on cassette* and, thus, anything embarrassing that I might accidentally say could be edited out.

I smiled my long-tooth-smile again.

The producer fixed her eyes hard on me and repeated, "Cassette."

. . . I repeated my nod and my smile.

"You know cassettes?" she asked.

I couldn't believe that she would think I didn't, so I returned a puzzled look.

Then she repeated, upped volume, lowered speed, "Cassettes. You have cassettes?"

Finally, I realized what she was asking. She wanted to know if I, having arrived from Jacksonville, Florida, had ever heard of cassettes.

I politely reassured her that I had cassettes.

Elsewhere, everywhere I have gone throughout the country, everyone has always assumed that I know cassettes.

I fear that you are worried about receiving irate letters from people in the South, the Midwest, and the West concerning your excerpt from FROM THE MIXED-UP FILES OF MRS. BASIL E. FRANKWEILER. I can only ask you to trust us out here . . . Everyone out here assumes that everyone knows about cassettes, Sara Lee pound cake and flush toilets, and we all assume about each other that we use each as the occasion and/or need arise.

Something in me does not want to believe that an editorial board at [your company] is as provincial as a provincial New Yorker.

I stand with Claudia and Jamie firmly on the toilets in the booths of the ladies' and men's rooms at the Metropolitan Museum of Art. Won't you please join us?

Sincerely. . . Elaine L. Konigsburg

There followed two phone calls.

The first was from the woman to whom I had addressed the letter. She told me that they had had several conferences about the toilets, and they were afraid that they would get irate letters from people. It was such a short passage. Wouldn't I consider letting them take it out?

I said no.

There followed that very morning a second phone call from the editor of the editor of the Department of Reading Basics. She said that there was a question of safety involved. That some child might read about standing on the toilets and try it and fall in.

I told her that I didn't believe that.

I mentioned that the book has been read by hundreds—probably even thousands—of children over the years, and I had never heard of anyone's falling into a toilet as a result of reading my book.

I told her that I had been to places in Kenya and China where the only way you could use it was to stand on it.

She said that she would confer again about the toilets and call me back.

Well, she didn't.

Instead I got this letter from Jean Karl.

Dear Elaine:

You will be interested to know that since you will not allow the children not to stand on the toilets [the publisher] has decided not to use the selection. I think they are being absurd and hope it doesn't bother you too much that they won't be using it.

Sincerely . . . etc. Jean Karl

This particular publisher has a trade book division that has been a pioneer in bringing toilets into the living room—so to speak. But what keeps the textbook division back a whole generation?

Fear.

Fears not too different from the ones I wrote about in my letter to them, for they are lusting after state adoptions of their sixth-grade reader. Four states—California, North Carolina, Texas, and Florida—of the twenty-three that have state adoption policies control over 50 percent of the textbook market. Therefore, departments of reading basics desire not to reach home. They desire to reach a market. They do not want to reach kids. They want to reach committees. So, they reason, the textbook that will be acceptable in Northern California is not the same one that will be acceptable in Orange County, California, and is still different from the one that will be acceptable in Bible Belt North Carolina. So let's just *bland* this up. Let our textbook be specific to no one, to nowhere. We'll offend no one, but we will sell books. We will sell lots of books. Hundreds—hundreds of thousands—of books.

So there is the editor—I hope a dying breed of editor—who can get between the hitter and the hittee in a book that is trying to reach home.

There is also the book critic. Children's books are in a special category because there are many more detours that a children's book must take before it can get into the hands of the child. This is changing with the increased availability of paperbacks, but the book critic still stands with the editor between the book and its reader. The book critic in the children's book field for a long time has been the librarian or the teacher, someone who works with children. But, alas, that is changing. I say *alas* because I feel that when the critics become full-time, they lose sight of home.

Let me explain.

In the field of adult books, there are many critics who have long ago lost sight of the reader. They begin to review for one another. They have ceased being a service. They have become a self-service.

For a long time it has been the opinion of these critics that serious writers will have nothing to do with plot. It is their further opinion that all serious writing must be solemn and needs only two elements: *style* and something called *a point of view.*

Mr. Louis Auchincloss, defending *The French Lieutenant's Woman* by John Fowles, wrote a reply to critics of the book that was published in the *New York Times Book Review* of February 1, 1970:

> I have always thought that one of the greatest problems a regular literary critic has to face is the effect on him of having to read more novels than could be expected of any normal man in his right senses. It seems to me that an almost inevitable consequence of this overdose would be to develop in him a greater need for innovation in the form of structure of the novel than would be felt by the lay reader. I am sure that if I had to read two or three novels a day, or even one, I would . . . [be] anxious to dispose of both plot and character as old fashioned devices.

## TalkTalk

One of the great joys of writing for children has been that the reviewers of children's books, unlike the reviewers of adult books, have kept in close touch with children, with readers who do not tire of plot and character. They have, in short, *gone home* to the reader to see if the book has been on target. And for a long time the same thing applied to people who serve on selection committees and award committees. But there is danger in the world of children's books and the danger is that those who review may have stopped going home, may have stopped having contact with children who read and have contact only with books and with other people—grown-up people—who select them. The worry is the librarian who because she is good is chosen for one committee and then another and then another, and soon she has contact with committees and not with children. She becomes someone who ceases *going home.*

—✦—

Home is really so many things. It is the place that we can hardly wait to leave, and it is the place we can hardly wait to come back to. It is the place that we must outgrow and yet the place that must always live within us. It is the place that we desperately need to escape and yet need always to return to. Home is something that helps create us when we are young, and yet it is something that we create when we are grown.

And a book is that for me. It is one kind of home as a writer and two other kinds as a reader. Books helped form me when I was young, and now that I am grown, I form them.

Since I write for children, I know that my books, my going-home books, are ones that my readers will outgrow just as my own children have outgrown home. But just as my children carry the ways of their home within them, I know that my readers will carry my books within them for a long, long time. I hope, too, that my readers will always feel comfortable—even feel a need for—returning home.

# The 70s (finito)

**P**ublic speaking gives a writer of children's books an opportunity to connect with an audience different from the one that reads her books.

After delivering "Going Home" to an audience in Jacksonville, Florida, I received a letter that I treasure as evidence that I had, indeed, connected. The letterhead reads: St. John's Cathedral; The Reverend Nathaniel W. Massey, Canon:

> Dear Mrs. Konigsburg,
>
> It was a privilege to be in your audience today. I thought, as you were speaking, about a traveler in England, about whom I once read. He (or she) was sure that they had been at the Inn at which they were staying. He asked his spouse and was assured they had never been at that place in England before. He knew the Inn and was sure he knew every bend in the stream behind the Inn. Then he remembered, *The Wind in the Willows.* He had come home.
>
> I am sure, as one who depends on words for a living, that the most important gift we can give a child is nurturing his ability to roam the world by the

printed page. Thank you for your writings and the
reason you write.
   I am
   Faithfully,
   Nathaniel W. Massey

—✛—

When the base of allowable subject matter and allowable language had sufficiently broadened, children's book writers were
able to consider previously forbidden subjects, and they did. The
result was a crop of "problem novels" for young adults. Every
good novel has a plot that sets out a problem that is solved in the
course of the story, but they are not necessarily problem novels.

In *Aspects of the Novel,* E. M. Forster distinguishes between
story and plot:

> Let us define a plot . . . "The king died and then the
> queen died" is a story. "The king died and then the
> queen died of grief" is a plot . . . Or again: "The
> queen died, no one knew why, until it was discovered
> that it was through grief at the death of the king."
> This is a plot with a mystery in it . . . Consider the
> death of the queen. If it is in a story we say "and
> then?" If it is in a plot we ask "why?" That is the fun-
> damental difference between these two aspects of the
> novel.

A story is not a sermon, and a plot is not a pulpit, but in a
problem novel, they are. Therein lies the fundamental difference between a novel that sets out a problem and a problem
novel.

In the 1670s, the plot of the problem novel would be:

> The fourteen-year-old died, no one knew why, until
> it was discovered she starved herself to death, and
> the devil made her do it.

In the 1770s, the plot would be:

> The fourteen-year-old died, no one knew why, until it was discovered that it was starvation by the British troops for refusing to give them information.

In the 1870s:

> The fourteen-year-old died, no one knew why, until it was discovered that it was starvation from being too lazy to work for a living.

In the 1970s:

> The sensitive, bright fourteen-year-old died, no one knew why, until it was discovered it was self-starvation brought on by feelings of inadequacy and rage in a high-achieving family. This disorder has a name: *anorexia nervosa*.

In the 1970s the problems of the problem novels all had proper names. Anorexia nervosa was a popular choice.

A problem novel describes the disease/disorder/disability and then the social/sexual/medical problem that results and then the diagnosis is made and then the discovery of a socially acceptable solution follows.

"If it is in a story we say 'and then?' If it is in a plot we ask 'why?'"

Plot is the thickening given to story. Plot makes visible the invisible. Plot reveals the hidden motive, the workings of the characters' minds. As I see it, the principle problem of growing up is hidden. It is the conflict between self-absorption and self-doubt. It is the malaise brought on by wanting two contradictory things: to be like everyone else and to be different from everyone else. And the essential plot of the novel for the middle-aged child resolves the conflict by finding a path between the two.

Just as I have been able to see myself moving deeper into the world of children's literature by standing farther back from it, I knew I could move deeper into plot by moving it farther back in time. It was then that I wrote two historical novels: *A Proud Taste for Scarlet and Miniver* in 1973 and *The Second Mrs. Giaconda* in 1975.

I moved into more recent history when I wrote *Father's Arcane Daughter,* a story that deals with the effects on a healthy older brother of living with a handicapped sibling. The handicap in my novel has no name. I had known the story, but in developing the plot, I moved it back to a time and place where I had lived–the 1950s in Pittsburgh, Pennsylvania–to help make my perspective clearer and my thinking deeper.

(*Father's Arcane Daughter* was made into the Emmy Award–winning Hallmark Hall of Fame production called *Caroline?*. In its transfer to the TV screen, the story was transformed again. Seeing one of my books made into a movie or into a television show is like seeing my children married: different version, different venue, but still blessedly and recognizably mine.)

Writers of problem novels always deal with "and then's," but they do not deal with "the king died and then the queen died" because they do not deal with royalty at all but with people plucked out of the ordinary population. Moving into the past seemed a healthy way to write of real problems without novelizing the TV Movie of the Week or plumbing the psychologist's handbook of case studies.

The first of these historical novels, *A Proud Taste for Scarlet and Miniver,* begins with a queen who is in heaven waiting for her king. The two speeches that follow explain how I plotted my way to "the queen died," and in the first, that queen was a most remarkable woman, Eleanor of Aquitaine.

# 5. The Middle-Aged Child Is Not an Oxymoron

When I received that first great letter of acceptance from my editor, Jean Karl, I was told that my book, *Jennifer, Hecate, Macbeth, William McKinley and Me, Elizabeth,* would be part of their spring list of novels for the middle-aged child. That was the first that I had ever heard of the term, *middle-aged child,* and I found it ridiculous. I couldn't think of a more contradictory set of terms than *middle-aged* and *child.*

*Life* magazine ran this cover in 1972 and stopped publishing a weekly edition ten weeks later.

But I don't think this cover did it.

By the time they ran this story about the middle-aged child I had come to accept the term the way a person accepts an unloved given name: he adapts it to himself. To *Life* magazine, the middle-aged child meant a child from six to twelve. To the publishing world, the middle-aged child spans the ages eight to twelve—a child whose reading habits are post–Dr. Seuss but pre–*The Sensuous Woman*. The child rated G through PG-13.

My adoption of the term *middle-aged child* has been helped by my establishing a relationship between the child, ages eight through twelve, and the Middle Ages. I mean the Middle Ages of Western civilization, those dark centuries of history from the time of the collapse of the Roman Empire until that great rebirth, the Renaissance.

I have not always been comfortable in the Middle Ages. I have not always had great respect for them as an era in our civilization. My thinking about them had been that they were those "one thousand years without a bath," a time when minds were as stiff as the armor considered their trademark. I thought of them as a period in history when people were bound to a role in life, generation after generation, a time when birth, not ability, determined what one could do. I thought of them as downright un-American. And they were.

Of course they were.

We had no Middle Ages in the New World. When knighthood was in flower in Europe and China, civilization in the Americas was still in the Bronze Age.

American history moved directly from infancy to adolescence. As a nation we skipped being middle-aged children. I am sorry we did, for I have come to love a great deal about that period of history since I have come to see a relationship between the middle-aged child and the Middle Ages. But just as I do not love everything about the middle-aged child, I do not love everything about the Middle Ages. But there are some aspects of both that I admire a great deal.

I would like to explain the evolution of those two loves and the relationship I perceive between them.

—✛—

There is in New York a branch of the Metropolitan Museum of Art called the Cloisters. It is located in a park on a high bluff overlooking the Hudson River. The Cloisters is unique in two ways: it is the only museum in the United States devoted exclusively to medieval art, and it is the only one that incorporates its artifacts into the structure of the building itself. For example:

This thirteenth-century doorway, through which one enters the Langon Chapel, was moved from a monastery church in Burgundy. Stonework of the chapel itself came from a church near Bordeaux.

Stained glass windows made during the Middle Ages were installed into the walls of the Cloisters.

When we lived in suburban New York, I took my children there often, for it was one of the few places in the city to which I had the courage to drive because I didn't have to travel through Manhattan traffic, and the museum grounds provided parking for timid drivers like me. Besides, it is a beautiful place.

One of the works of art that fascinated my son Paul was a wooden rosary bead. It was a giant as far as rosary beads go—about the size of a golf ball. It was hinged, and the curators chose to display it opened. There, within that tiny realm, was carved a three-dimensional scene of Christ's Crucifixion. The medieval artist had found space to carve Mary, Joseph of Arimathea, and troops of Roman soldiers. The whole carving is so exquisite that one can read the expressions on the faces of the people, faces no bigger than a seed of allspice or clove.

My son was so impressed with this bead that he decided to carve one for his favorite teacher. At the moment, his favorite teacher was Mrs. Helene Braver, his Hebrew teacher. He knew that she would appreciate a scene of Moses on Mt. Sinai more than she would appreciate Christ on Golgotha. So that was the scene he decided upon. He borrowed a paring knife from me and stole a small piece of pine from a construction site near our home and went to work.

There you have the mind of a middle-aged child—he was eight at the time. He wanted to carve a rosary bead for a teacher of Hebrew. He wanted to do something beautiful, and he stole to do it. His thinking was truly Middle Aged or medieval. The contradictions existed side by side. There was no blending of the right of what he wanted to do with the wrong of it. They existed side by side. There was no blending of the concepts of Christian and Jew. For him, *Jewish* and *rosary bead* existed side by side.

On a visit to a different museum with a different child, I witnessed another aspect of the confluence of the medieval mind and that of the middle-aged child.

The J. P. Morgan Library in New York houses hundreds of famous manuscripts. Many of these treasures are hand-printed, hand-painted works on parchment that were completed from the time before the invention of the printing press. (The invention of the printing press is one possible way of marking the beginning of the end of the Middle Ages.) These manuscripts are shown to the public a few at a time. During one exhibit, the Library displayed pages from the Book of Hours of Catherine of Cleves, a fifteenth-century volume of prayers and psalms. Pages of hand-lettered text with illuminated letters and hand-painted miniatures with elaborate borders filled the display cases.

One of the miniatures—a picture no bigger than the palm of my hand—was one of

God creating Eve.

Here is Adam in the buff, lying on his side, as nonchalant as you please, his head turned in God's direction, while a woman—full-grown and as naked as Adam himself—unfolds from his side. God is barefoot but dressed like a medieval king.

In the time I spent in that museum, I watched a little girl return to that picture four times. The little girl was middle-aged. She was ten. She was my daughter.

Of course she was fascinated.

Here is a literal interpretation of Genesis 2:21–22.

And the rib, which the Lord God had taken from the man, made He a woman.

The middle-aged child listens literally and interprets literally. My daughter was as comfortable with that picture as she was with pictures of David killing Goliath with a slingshot or with this picture of

the mouth of hell

from that same Book of Hours. The mouth of hell is literally depicted as a mouth, and the fires of hell are bright licks of flame.

This literal translation is not too different from a story related by a friend of mine.

In the long-ago days before gay pride, she took her ten-year-old daughter to the hairdresser for a haircut. The child settled in the chair, and before the gentleman holding the scissors could begin, she turned around and with a smile that was beatific said, "I heard my daddy tell my mommy that you're a fairy, and I've never seen a real live fairy before."

Like the medieval mind, the mind of a middle-aged child prefers a literal interpretation.

It was at another museum, the Worcester Museum of Art, that I became a true believer in the term the *middle-aged child*. That museum was housing an exhibit of sculptures by Houdon, the great eighteenth-century artist to whom we owe our most accurate images of Voltaire and George Washington. His work was so accurate that measurements of his statue of Lafayette were used to identify the hero's bones. As I was taking in the exhibit, a class came through. They stood in front of a statue of George Washington. Before the docent could begin her lecture, one little girl pointed to the statue and asked, "How did he die?" The docent did not answer. They moved on to the next statue. The same little girl pointed again and asked again, "How did he die?" The same thing happened at the next. And the one after that. I found out from their teacher, who was watching from the sidelines, that they were a class of fourth-graders. Nine- and ten-year-olds. They were middle-aged children, and they were concerned with death.

The Middle Ages were also concerned with death.

People went to great expense to prepare for it. They built monumental crypts and awe-inspiring tombs to commemorate death. Every Book of Hours has as a standard feature the Book of the Dead. It was not until the Middle Ages that the Crucifixion gained popularity as a suitable subject for works of religious art. Prior to the Middle Ages, it was the Resurrection, not the pain of Christ's death, that was stressed.

That is still the case in the Greek Orthodox faith, the Eastern church where feudalism was less completely developed.

Once I recognized these basic parallels, I easily found others.

Look at a painting or a piece of sculpture that was executed during the time of the Middle Ages, and it is hard to find perspective in the work. A middle-aged child lacks perspective in his philosophy as well as in his art. A middle-aged child outlines his pictures in bold black crayon and enthusiastically fills in the spaces with bold, bright color. Compare that to

this piece of thirteenth-century stained glass.

Even the spelling bears comparison. Chaucer spells *eat,* E-T-E, and the middle-aged child asks, "Well, if E-T-E doesn't spell *eat,* what in the world does it spell?"

Abiding, superseding–almost bellowing–over all this is faith. The people of the Middle Ages were believers. In ghosts, angels, and demons. And fairies. And so are middle-aged kids. The people of the Middle Ages traveled miles and miles to view the relics of Thomas Becket at Canterbury because they believed in the healing power of relics. How different is this from the good-luck ring worn by a child of ten?

By the time I was convinced that the term *middle-aged child* is not an oxymoron, I also felt comfortable with the Middle Ages. And then I went to see *Becket,* the play by Jean Anouilh that tells of the clash between Henry II, king of England, and Thomas Becket, the man he raised to be archbishop of Canterbury. I loved the play, but there was one jarring note in it. I returned home sufficiently bothered to consult an encyclopedia to get the facts.

Henry II was one of the all-time great kings of England. He

laid the foundation for the whole of English common law. He started a civil service, a corporate policy whereby men were chosen according to ability and paid in coin rather than land. He was a strong king, a powerful executive.

I have known a lot of executives in my time—and what is a medieval king but an executive in drag?—and I've known a lot of executive wives. Executive wives are strong women. To stay with a man of vitality and ego requires a woman of character. The executive wives I have known have a core of strength.

Listen to what Anouilh has written for the wife of Henry II; she is called the Young Queen in the play. In act 4 he has given her the following lines:

> . . . I am your wife and your Queen. I refuse to be treated like this! I shall complain to my father, the Duke of Aquitaine! I shall complain to my uncle, the Emperor! I shall complain to all the Kings of Europe, my cousins! I shall complain to God!

After I consulted the encyclopedia, I found out the Young Queen's father, the duke of Aquitaine, had died long before she married Henry, but that inaccuracy did not bother me. I also found out that her uncle was not the emperor but was the king of Jerusalem, but that did not bother me. All the kings of Europe were not her cousins, but that didn't matter. What mattered was the Young Queen's manner. It did not ring true. After I consulted the encyclopedia, I found out that the Young Queen was twelve years older than Henry—that did not matter either. She had a name; she was not simply *wife of.* She was not simply the *Young Queen.* She had a name, and she mattered. She was Eleanor. Eleanor of Aquitaine. I wanted to tell the playwright that Eleanor of Aquitaine may have been a bitch, but—let's give credit where it's due—she was a great one.

What started as a cursory examination became a passion.

What a woman! What a woman was Eleanor of Aquitaine.

At a time when a king-husband could keep his queen-wife in prison, and Henry did—he did that; he locked Eleanor up for fifteen years—at a time when women were considered chattel, Eleanor of Aquitaine was in essence everything that women's liberation was in slogans.

Eleanor of Aquitaine was the woman who was wife not to one king, but to two. She divorced Louis VII of France and married Henry of England. She was thirty at the time, and he was eighteen, and if that does not spell doing your own thing, what in the world does it spell?

Eleanor was rich. Richer than either of her two husbands. Richer than Henry when she married him. After their wedding, they traveled through the lands that he received from

her dowry. It was a medieval combination of honeymoon, political show-and-tell, and photo-op. It was during this trip that

this double portrait of her and Henry was sculpted in Langon near Bordeaux.

Now it can be seen on a column in the chapel at the Cloisters, just beyond that thirteenth-century doorway from Burgundy.

Eleanor of Aquitaine was the woman responsible for lifting a minor Saxon king by the name of Arthur from the dusty pages of a history book and handing him over to troubadours who imbued him with grace and chivalry, bedecked him with honor, and seated him at a Round Table with a band of noble, if sometimes lecherous, knights in shining armor. Eleanor of Aquitaine was the woman responsible for establishing the rules of courtly love, rules by which many of us grew up. Rules whose vestiges we witness when a man tips his hat or rises when a woman enters a room, or gives up his seat on a crowded bus.

Eleanor of Aquitaine was wife to two kings and mother of two. You know her sons by name. One lies under

this effigy in Worcester Cathedral. His name was John.

That same King John who signed a great charter at Runnymede in the year 1215.

Her other son was Richard the Lion-Hearted. He led the Third Crusade. He was captured on his way home. His English subjects paid—guess what?— a king's ransom to get him back. Do kids still use that term? Do they know where it came from?

Richard is buried in France. He lies on his mother's left at Fontevrault. His father, King Henry II, lies on her right. All three of them wear crowns. Henry and Richard hold scepters. Only Eleanor holds a book.

The lifetime of Eleanor of Aquitaine is a watershed. The years from 1122 to 1204 mark the time when the Crusades, perhaps the greatest cultural exchanges of all time, were at their peak. Hers was the time when the great universities were established. It was the time when the middle classes started their upward mobility. And European art was changing from

Romanesque

to Gothic.

I wanted to write about this queen for children. Most historical novels written for children invent a young character and plop him into the chosen era. Unless it is done well—as it is in *Johnny Tremain*—one can hear the splash. I didn't want to do that. Eleanor of Aquitaine already had an age—the middle ages—in common with the readers I wished to reach.

So I wrote a book of a bastard genre. Everyone who inhabits its pages has lived. They speak in phrases that are historically documented as well as others I invented. But there is over, under, and throughout this mixture of fact and fiction, and even some fantasy, a truth. A truth about a woman.

A truth about a woman of purpose. A woman of the Middle Ages linked to middle-aged children. I hope that when they meet Eleanor of Aquitaine in the pages of *A Proud Taste for Scarlet and Miniver,* they will come to love her as I have and to know themselves a little better for doing so.

# 6. Sprezzatura: A Kind of Excellence

When people ask me why I write for children, I usually give them the answers they most want to hear. For example, when the ladies-who-lunch ask me, I tell them that I write for children because it's so damn much fun. That's what they thought all along, anyway. I always add the damn because writers are supposed to be profane; writers for children are allowed to be only slightly profane so that's why I say *damn* instead of *goddamn*. When my in-laws who still refer to me as *whatsername* ask, I tell them that I write for children because I have a very limited vocabulary. They like that because it's what they believed all along, anyway. To a chance dinner partner, the gentleman at my left, the executive making polite dinner conversation with Dr. Konigsburg's wife, I say that I write for children because my husband won't allow me to write hardcore pornography. He likes to hear that; it means that, working woman though I am, the man of the family is still boss.

But today I would like to give all of you the smartest possible answer. Smartest because it is the real one, and I would like to tell you why I write for children by tracing the specific roots of my book called *The Second Mrs. Giaconda*.

The whispered beginnings of *The Second Mrs. Giaconda* go back to George Washington's birthday in 1963. Back in

1963, you could ask any schoolchild in the northeastern part of the United States where we then lived, "When was George Washington born?" and that schoolchild would tell you, "February 22, 1732." Nowadays, he would answer that George Washington was born on the third Monday of every February, and so was Abraham Lincoln.

Back in 1963, George Washington's birthday was a school holiday that fell during the period that the *Mona Lisa* was on loan from the Louvre in Paris to the Metropolitan Museum of Art in New York City. The grand lady was receiving, and I and my entire family were in the receiving line . . . behind a police barricade, in the cold twenty-five-degree air, stamping our feet to keep the blood moving because we certainly weren't. It took us forty-five minutes to climb the steps to get a glimpse of the picture. And we got just that—a glimpse—because once inside, we moved very fast. We were herded in and out, just a little slower—a little, mind you—than in and out of the doors of a rush-hour subway.

Considering the cold and hurried reception we got, my family vocalized on the way home about how Madonna Lisa wasn't worth the trip from New Jersey, let alone the trip from France. It had been my idea to go, so I spoke in self-defense and said, "Well, it was free."

My husband reminded me that even though entrance to the museum was free (at that time it still was) there was the matter of parking and bridge tolls, the five giant pretzels and the six bags of roasted chestnuts that we had managed to consume during that forty-five-minute climb up the stairs. I was quiet but resentful the rest of the way home and for years to come. I don't carry a grudge well, but I carry it forever. Or almost.

On October 25, 1965, the *New York Times* announced that the Metropolitan Museum of Art had acquired a wonderful bargain. For the sum of only $225, it had obtained at auction this plaster and stucco *Bust of a Lady.*

The newspaper said that this sculpture dated from the time of Leonardo da Vinci and might be his work or that of his teacher, Andrea del Verrocchio.

When I adapted that piece of information as well as the experience of waiting in line to see a famous work of art in my book *From the Mixed-up Files of Mrs. Basil E. Frankweiler,* I changed the possible authorship of the mystery statue from Leonardo to Michelangelo. Because I had never had to wait in line to see a work of his on loan from France.

In 1967 the National Gallery of Art in Washington, D.C., paid a record $5 million for

this portrait of *Ginevra de'Benci,* the only painting by Leonardo in the United States.

Some art critics questioned if Ginevra were worth it, and I did, too, until I went to Washington and saw for myself what has given a lot of pleasure to a lot of eyes for five hundred years.

Now we're up to 1969, the year of my maiden trip to Italy. The trip was a Michelangelo pilgrimage, really, but there in the Uffizi, I came within an arm's length of two of Leonardo's paintings I had often seen in reproduction. One of them, the *Annunciation,* held me spellbound. There is a freshness in that painting that one experiences after a summer rain in a temperate zone, a feeling of newness that almost eerily suits the mood of an annunciation.

## TalkTalk

When we went to Milan, we visited the refectory of Santa Maria delle Grazie. There, gazing at that wall, it happened again.

There in the presence of Leonardo's magnificent ruin of *The Last Supper,* I once again felt touched by magic.

This was magic powerful enough to overcome—even overwhelm—all the triteness that comes from the myriad copies and roadside interpretations done on black velvet.

I stood there in the refectory and wanted to bite my tongue for a remark I had made at a friend's house. Sitting in her dining room, facing the wall on which hung just such a reproduction, I had nudged my dinner partner and said, "Caption: Separate checks, please."

If trite reproductions inspire sarcasm, the work itself inspires awe.

—✦—

What quality does Leonardo have that comes to us from the original work and not from reproductions? Something besides size shrinks when his work is reproduced. Something organic is lost when his work is reduced and reproduced.

I returned from that trip to Italy with respect but not yet love for Leonardo. New loves come slowly in middle age. But love came. And the vehicle of love was a book I bought at an estate sale. A friend who is an antique dealer was given the contents of an estate to dispose of. The sale had to be private and by appointment because the property belonged to the wife of a man whose name is infamous; his brother had committed murder fifty years before in a case so famous that the books and plays and movies it has spawned will not let the details or the names die.

I found my way into the study, and there, all alone, I pored over the books. All the lovely coffee-table books were being sold by size. The largest were four dollars apiece. I bought several, one of which was called *The Horizon Book of the Renaissance.* In that book I found an essay that led first to love of Leonardo and then to a book about him.

The essay was written by the scientist Jacob Bronowski. In it Bronowski speculates that at the age of thirty-one Leonardo left Florence and went to Milan because he was uneasy in the rarefied, super-snobbish intellectual atmosphere that prevailed in the Florence of the Medici. Leonardo was not a bookish man; he was not a person who believed in ideas instead of observation. His notebooks contain a heated defense of his beliefs, written with an almost adolescent scorn for men who are very bookish. Leonardo calls men fools who will not trust their own senses.

Leonardo needed approval. He needed admiration, and he was not emotionally equipped to fight it out in Florence, so he chose to go to Milan, where he had less competition, where he was indisputably the maestro.

Bronowski's article made Leonardo something more than a genius; it made him a human genius. Every great love requires some imperfection, and Leonardo's pride was a weakness that I found endearing.

I began to study Leonardo's life and his work, and I would

like to take you now to where that study took me. It took me ultimately to the question with which I begin *The Second Mrs. Giaconda*.

> Why, people ask, why did Leonardo da Vinci choose to paint the portrait of the second wife of an unimportant Florentine merchant when dukes and duchesses all over Italy and the King of France as well, were all begging for a portrait by his hand? Why, they ask, why?
> The answer lies with Salai.

Yes, Salai. You must meet him, but before you do, let me set the stage.

Come with me.

Come with me now to Milan in the year 1492. I picked the year 1492 because it was a very good year. If you remember your history, Columbus discovered America on the second Monday of every October of that year.

Let me introduce you to some of the people that you and Barbara Walters would have enjoyed meeting at the court of Milan.

First, there was the duke of Milan. His name was Ludovico Sforza, and he was forty years old.

He was also called Il Moro because his complexion was dark, and he resembled a Moor. Like Othello. Like Othello, he was an excellent lover and soldier. He rose to his position not through a direct line of descent but through an L-shaped move and maybe a few judicious murders. But, remember, this was the age of Machiavelli, and Il Moro was a product of his times.

Il Moro's court, the court of Milan, was rich.

Richer than Florence. Its riches were newer; it was nouveau riche, a bit too lavish in its display and a bit too loud in its self-celebration. The court of Milan stood to the city of Florence as Los Angeles stands to the city of New York: more spread out, flashier, more experimental, and just a little defensive about being so.

But this duke, this Il Moro, had an eye for quality. He was a fine patron of the arts. Not only did he have fine taste and vast powers of organization, but he was always open to new ideas. Capable of minute attention to detail, he also gave rein to talent.

Milan under the rule of Il Moro was proclaimed the new Athens. It is no wonder that Leonardo stayed there for seventeen years. There will always be those who in the history of the Renaissance regard Il Moro as a parvenu, but then, there are always those who regard the Kennedys of Massachusetts as parvenu compared to the Cabots and the Lodges.

I mentioned that in addition to being a fine soldier and an excellent patron of the arts, Il Moro was also a fine lover. In 1492 he was in love with this beautiful lady.

Her name was Cecilia Gallerani. Il Moro had Leonardo paint this portrait of her.

Beautiful, intelligent, and accomplished. She must have been quite a woman to have Il Moro fall in love with her because at the time, he still qualified as a bridegroom.

Only a year before, Il Moro had been married. His wife was young—very young—only seventeen. She was small and dark and plain.

Her maiden name was Beatrice d'Este. She was the second daughter of the duke and duchess of Ferrara.

Beatrice had an older sister whose name was Isabella. Her mother and father had not minded when their first child was a girl. After all, their first-born was beautiful and talented and precocious, and they felt certain that sons would follow. What followed was Beatrice, small and dark and plain.

When Beatrice was still a baby, her mother, the beautiful Leonora, took her two daughters on a visit to her father, the king of Naples. She returned to Ferrara, leaving Beatrice, but not Isabella, in Naples. She collected Beatrice later—eight years later. It appears that even during the Renaissance blondes had more fun.

Perhaps such parental neglect was good after all. There were at least those eight years in which Beatrice did not grow up in the shadow of her blonde and beautiful sister.

It was Isabella, not Beatrice, who Il Moro had wanted to marry. When Isabella was a mere child, he had traveled to Ferrara, and as was the custom at the time, asked for her hand in marriage. But he was a little too late. Just two weeks before, she had been promised to Francesco Gonzaga, the marquis of Mantua, a much younger man. So Il Moro, anxious to cement political ties with the house of Ferrara, consented to marry Beatrice instead.

Poor, pitiful Beatrice. Married to a man twenty-three years

her senior. A man in love with another woman. No sooner had their wedding ceremony been performed than the bridegroom left his bride at the church in the company of her mother and sister. Saying that he had to arrange for her reception, he rushed back to Milan.

Cecilia was in Milan.

Poor, plain Beatrice. Second daughter, second choice, second thought.

Now meet Isabella d'Este. She has been called the First Lady of the Renaissance.

Since she was always commissioning poets, it is entirely possible that the phrase was a designated title. Isabella was acquisitive and spoiled. She was an accumulator rather than a collector.

Leonardo did this charcoal drawing of her, but she could never get him to commit it to oils even though she nagged and nagged by letter and messenger. She was an inveterate letter writer.

Allow me to present one of her letters and one of Beatrice's replies. They reveal a lot about the two sisters.

In the first, Isabella is writing to her husband:

> Most Illustrious Lord:
> Your excellency has desired me to send the four pieces of drapery that belonged to the French king, in order that you may present them to my sister, the Duchess of Milan. I, of course, obey you, but in this instance I must say I do it with great reluctance, as I think these royal spoils ought to remain in our family, in perpetual memory of your glorious deeds, of which we have no other record. By giving them to others you appear to surrender the honor of the enterprise with these trophies of the victory. I do not

send them today because they require a mule, and I
also hope that you will be able to make some excuse
to the duchess and tell her, for instance that you have
already given me these hangings. If I had not seen
them already, I should not have cared so much, but
since you gave them to me in the first place, and they
were won at the peril of your own life, I shall only
give them up with tears in my eyes. All the same, as I
said before, I will obey your excellency, but shall
hope to receive some explanation in reply. If these
draperies were a thousand times more valuable than
they are, and had they been acquired in any other
way, I should gladly give them up to my sister the
duchess, whom, as you know, I love and honor with
all my heart. But under the circumstances, I must
own it is very hard for me to part with them.

You see, they had sibling rivalry in the Renaissance; they just
hadn't heard of it.

Beatrice showed herself, as she habitually did, to be the
more generous of the two. Beatrice, having duly received and
admired her brother-in-law's gifts, sent them back to Mantua
with the following note:

I have today received, by your Highness's courier,
the drapery belonging to the King of France . . .
I thank you exceedingly, but I feel that, under the
circumstances, I ought not to keep them. As it is,
I have great pleasure in seeing them all together,
and now your Highness can give them back to the
Marchesana.

So there was Beatrice after her marriage, a bride overshadowed by her husband's beautiful mistress as she had been
overshadowed at home by her sister. But then something
happened. Something strange and wonderful and terribly,
terribly romantic. Sometime after he married her, Il Moro
fell in love with his wife.

It is recorded fact. Letters tell how attentive he became to her, how he spoke endearments and kissed her in public. But why? What made him appreciate her? What made him send Cecilia packing, off to marry Count Bergamini?

Leonardo was in Milan when the duke fell in love with his wife. Knowing the influence of Leonardo on the tastes and manners and style of those who dealt with him, I couldn't dismiss his presence in the court of Milan as being entirely passive. Leonardo was there, and so was Giacomo Salai.

Salai is the beautiful young man on the right side of this page from Leonardo's records. He appears often in Leonardo's notebooks, where he is drawn in both words and pictures.

Leonardo wrote, "Giacomo came to live with me on St. Mary Magdalene's day 1490, aged ten years." He goes on to relate Salai's misdeeds during the first few days of his apprenticeship, and then in the margin, he wrote: *thief, liar, obstinate, glutton.* From that entry forward there are scattered accounts of Salai's many misdemeanors.

Yet Leonardo never gave up on him. He kept this Salai with him for more than twenty years, helped pay his sister's dowry, and remembered him in his will.

Why? Why did Leonardo do that?

There is an easy explanation: Leonardo da Vinci was a homosexual. His relationship with Salai was, as Kenneth Clark so delicately put it, "of the kind honored in classical times, and partly tolerated in the Renaissance in spite of the censure of the Church."

But, you see, I am glad that I write for children. For that explanation of his use of a young man will never do. Never do altogether. It is simply not enough. It is not deep enough. It does not tell the whole truth. If I were writing for adults at this moment in our American literary history, I would concoct a sordid, fast-paced tale about this relationship. But I know that writing for children requires a deeper truth. You cannot explain a twenty- or twenty-five-year relationship on the basis of sex alone. Anyone who has been married for even half that length of time knows that. Long relationships that withstand annoyances and independent bad habits and that stand up to the minute-by-minute—not the year-by-year—of living together are based on mutual need.

What would Leonardo need? What could Salai supply to Leonardo's life? Leonardo, the complete, the total, the Renaissance man?

Study his scientific work, and I venture you will come away more impressed by his gadgets than his genius. (You see another reason why I am glad I write for children: I can approach the work of Leonardo da Vinci as they do—unshackled by a feeling of awe.) Genius always makes quantum leaps.

Upon taking up residence in Milan, Leonardo started his notebooks. Did he get lost in the details? He looked at things in a totally accurate way, for I believe he was the world's greatest observer, but did he become so much the empiricist, so much the anti-Platonist that he would never generalize? Did he become too much the tinkerer, too little the thinker? Did Leonardo become too inhibited to make a quantum leap?

What was lacking in his ultimate design of the statue of the bronze horse, his great commission for Il Moro? He worked on it on and off for sixteen years. Il Moro sent the metal to a relative to be used for cannon, so it was never cast in bronze, but a full-scale plaster model appeared more massive than majestic. Could that be because Leonardo got too busy working out a mathematical system for the proportions of the anatomy of the horse using fractions of 1/900?

Leonardo made a quantum leap in art. Not always. But often. Why did some of his works of art possess the quality of genius and others, not?

What is lacking, for example, in this, his last painting, *St. John the Baptist?* Why an inhibited, self-conscious, androgynous St. John?

Something is missing. I think I know what.

A wild element is missing. Everything is too tight and too controlled. Nothing swings.

Every great work of art, every work of genius, has a wild element. Some artists carry that wild element within them. Michelangelo did. Rembrandt did. Beethoven did. But Leonardo did not.

Leonardo, the bastard son, the self-educated, defensive, self-conscious, inhibited genius, needed Salai. He needed Salai to supply the irreverence, the wild element, the all-important something awful that great works of art have. The controlled Leonardo needed Salai's recklessness. Salai also gave Leonardo a necessary sense of unimportance. We all need a child to do that. In many ways Salai was a perpetual child.

In the court of Milan Leonardo was employed by Il Moro on many projects. He was Il Moro's resident wizard: Design a war machine, Maestro Leonardo. Design costumes for a pageant, Maestro. Paint the ceilings in my new rooms; paint a wall in the refectory; paint a portrait of my very good friend, the lovely Madonna Cecilia Gallerani.

Leonardo did those things. And after Ludovico and Beatrice

had been married a few years, and Beatrice was pregnant with their third child, Il Moro called Leonardo to him and requested that he paint another portrait. A portrait of one Lucrezia Crivelli, Il Moro's new mistress. Leonardo painted Lucrezia.

He painted the ceiling, and he painted the wall of the refectory; he painted portraits of Il Moro's mistresses, but for all the years he remained in Milan, Leonardo never, never painted a portrait of poor, dear Beatrice. He did a sketch of her sister Isabella, but he never, never painted Beatrice.

Why?

Why did he never paint Beatrice?

Beatrice died at the age of twenty-two, but there had been time enough before she died for him to have painted her. Her early death was not the reason.

Shortly after Beatrice died, Milan was invaded by the French, and Ludovico was exiled. Leonardo went to Florence, stopping en route in Mantua to visit Isabella. It was then that he did the charcoal drawing of her.

When he returned to Florence after having been away for seventeen years, his reputation, partly as a result of the success of *The Last Supper*, was at its peak. He was bombarded with requests for paintings. Kings, bishops, princes, and princesses—most especially Duchess Isabella—were begging for a portrait from his hand.

He promised them all, and he delivered to none.

Yet, during these years back in Florence, he spent three years painting the second wife of an unimportant Florentine merchant. He did the work entirely by himself, allowing no apprentice hand to touch it.

This is the point, the question with which I begin my book, *The Second Mrs. Giaconda*. "Why, people ask, why did Leonardo da Vinci choose to paint the second wife of an unimportant Florentine merchant . . ."

## E.L. Konigsburg

Look at her. Look at Madonna Lisa Giaconda.

Can you look at her without awe? Can you look at her without feeling bored by the countless reproductions of her face? Can you look at her without resenting having to wait in line outside the Metropolitan Museum of Art on a cold February day?

If you are lucky enough to write books for children, you have a chance for a fresh look at her. You have a chance to introduce some unjaded, but awe-free, young appetites to the mysteries of this lady. What a joy to write for young people who are not weary of seeing her.

This is a woman who knows that she is not pretty and has learned to live with that knowledge. This is a woman whose acceptance of herself has made her beautiful in a deep and hidden way. A woman whose look tells you that you are being sized by an invisible measuring rod in her head, a measuring rod on which she alone has etched the units. A woman who knows how to endure. A woman of layers. A woman whose very unimportance allowed Leonardo to swing loose and free with the composition.

Is she possibly what Beatrice would have become had she lived? She was just the age that Beatrice would have been had she lived. Is this possibly the portrait of Beatrice that Leonardo never painted? A possible surrogate Beatrice without the royal clothes and regal jewelry?

—✛—

Young readers give me what Salai gave Leonardo: a highly developed sense of unimportance. We match up quite well. Just as Salai lacked reverence toward important works, so do young readers. They provide me with the necessary wild

**113**

element. And that is why they are a challenge to write for. And because they are that challenge, I like to write for them.

Now, when you ask why I write for children, I will tell you that writing for them makes me research history and human emotions. Writing for children makes me research deeply, beyond and beneath the slick, sexy reasons that lie on the surface.

And writing for children demands a certain kind of excellence: the quality that Salai helped to give Leonardo, the quality that young readers demand in their books as Renaissance viewers demanded it in their art. A quality that says that all works of art must have weight and knowing beneath them, that a work of art must have all the techniques and the skills—it must never be sloppy—but it must never, never, for God's sake, never show the gears. Make it nonchalant, easy. Make it light. The men of the Renaissance called that kind of excellence *sprezzatura.*

And because Salai appreciated it, Leonardo kept him with him. And because children demand it subliminally and appreciate it loudly, and because I do, too, that is why I write for children.

# Into the 80s

Ever since I have been writing books, whenever and wherever and to whomever I speak, the first question asked of me is: Where do you get your ideas? Writers are always asked that.

Except for a year at boarding school as a teenager, one trip to Washington, D.C., and a couple of visits to eye doctors in Boston, Emily Dickinson spent every day of her life in Amherst, Massachusetts. She spent her time at home reading, baking cookies, and writing letters and some of the most beautiful poetry in our language. Amherst, Massachusetts, was *where* her ideas came from, her only *where*.

Ernest Hemingway hunted big game in Africa, fished for marlin in the waters of the Gulf Stream, watched bullfights in Spain, drove an ambulance in Italy during World War I, walked away from an airplane crash, won a Nobel Prize for literature, divorced three times, married four, and committed suicide because he had no *where* to go as a writer.

When I am asked where I get my ideas, I respond by relating an anecdote or telling about something I read or observed that triggered a story, and what I tell is true.

It is also not true.

Anyone who has experienced creative insight—whether in the world of science or the world of art—knows that the *where* of where ideas come from is *inside your head*.

For example, many people saw the same great block of Carrara marble that Michelangelo saw. As a matter of fact, someone had already chipped away at it before Michelangelo got to it, but it was only Michelangelo who saw a giant statue of David in that stone. In the nineteenth century, a lot of people knew as much about the chemistry of benzene as did Friedrich August Kekulé, but it was he who got the idea for the carbon ring structure of benzene. A lot of geneticists were privy to the same information about chromosomes and DNA that Watson and Crick were privy to, but it was they who got the idea for the double helix. A lot of people have Jewish mothers, but only Philip Roth made a Mrs. Portnoy out of that raw material.

Raw material is all around all the time.

For the novelist or poet, for the scientist or artist, the question is not *where* do ideas come from, the question is how they come. The *how* is the mystery. The how is fragile.

The how is related to time, to the chronology of time. All advances in the world of science or art depend on what has gone before. Watson and Crick could not have discovered the structure of DNA if someone had not discovered X-ray diffraction first. But ideas depend not only upon chronology but also upon the tenor of the times, for genius does not always live in the age it deserves.

What if Michelangelo had signed a contract for that giant block of Carrara marble in 1301 instead of 1501? In 1301 the city of Florence was a confused and gloomy battleground for the Black Guelphs and the White Guelphs, the Democrats and Republicans of their day. But on September 13, 1501, when Michelangelo started his work, Florence was a republic that wanted a work of art that would express its civic pride. So out of the giant block of Carrara marble, Michelangelo carved a statue of David, noble, heroic, and naked.

Had Michelangelo signed his contract in September of 1301 or September of 1901, David might be noble and he might be heroic, but he would not be naked, for creative acts depend upon not only what has gone before but also what is current. Excellence is subject to fashion.

When the heart and the mind of a writer are out of sync with his times, either his book will go unpublished or unappreciated. Earlier I mentioned how in *Up From Jericho Tel.* I explored how important timing is to success in the arts, and how important it was to the publication and success of my first book. My heart and my head were in the right place at the right time. The X-ray diffraction of children's books had been invented. The republic of publishing was ready, and so was I. I saw the statue in the stone. I was ready to transform an idea into a book. The constraints without were gone. I needed only to undo the constraints within.

Between the imagination and the image—of a molecule of DNA, or a Jewish mother, or a mathematical model—the idea has to be set free. And some conditions help to set it free.

—✝—

In 1983 I was asked to address the Fifth Biennial Institute in Children's Literature at Simmons College. The theme for the institute was "Do I Dare Disturb the Universe?" Their brochure outlining the schedule and participants explained:

> The theme is taken from T. S. Eliot's "The Love Song of J. Alfred Prufrock." . . . Investigative in nature, the Institute will . . . address questions which go beyond the common round—questions of action and inaction . . .

In some way, every creative action disturbs the universe.

Investigating how creative ideas are translated into action goes beyond the question, "Where do you get your ideas?" The lambent mystery of *how* remains, but I could investigate what it takes to set ideas free from the hearts and minds of writers.

The result is "Between a Peach and the Universe."

# 7. Between a Peach and the Universe

When I was a sophomore at Carnegie Mellon University, I studied T. S. Eliot, and I studied calculus.

Well, T. S. Eliot has made it to Broadway, and calculus hasn't.

But I must confess that when I was in college, I would not have been surprised if calculus had made it instead. For at that time, I thought that the poetry of Mr. Eliot was every bit as arcane as calculus.

Upon returning home from seeing a performance of *Cats,* I opened my sophomore textbook, *Chief Modern Poets of England & America,* and I saw tucked between its pages a verse of "The Rum Tum Tugger," complete with notes that make no sense at all, in a hand I do not recognize.

> The Rum Tum Tugger is a curious beast:
> His disobliging ways are a matter of habit.
> If you offer him a fish then he always wants
>   a feast;
> When there isn't any fish then he won't eat
>   rabbit.

Here are my notes: Rum Tum Tugger and beast are underlined, and in the margin beside that line, I have written "Lion of Judah." Beside the line, "If you offer him a fish then he

**118**

always wants a feast," I have written, "Miracle of loaves and fishes." And scribbled in the margin beside the line, "When there isn't any fish then he won't eat rabbit," there is a note to the effect that Catholics don't eat meat on Fridays. (During my sophomore year in college, that was a matter of habit.)

On Broadway, T. S. Eliot's *Cats* appeared to be pretty uncomplicated. I wondered if at Carnegie Mellon, I or my teacher, Mr. John Hart, had been reading a bit too much between the lines. Dr. Hart was one of a group of professors who met once a week to read and discuss a single page of *Ulysses* by James Joyce, and I was, God forgive me, a sophomore.

After studying "The Rum Tum Tugger," I read the textbook section on T. S. Eliot and found "The Love Song of J. Alfred Prufrock." I remembered liking that poem for its rhythm.

> Let us go then, you and I,
> When the evening is spread out against the sky
> Like a patient etherized upon a table;

I will spare you what I have written in the margin beside "etherized upon a table." As I continued reading, I stopped trying to decipher my notes—which were marginal in both the literal and figurative senses of the word—and I began to read the poem straight through. I found myself saying, "Yes, I understand," and "Yes, I don't." Not, "No, I don't understand," but "*Yes,* I don't." Saying *yes, I don't understand* is a privilege that comes either with religious faith or old age.

At last I came to these lines:

> And indeed there will be time
> To wonder, "Do I dare?" and "Do I dare?"
> . . . . . . . . . . .
> Do I dare
> Disturb the universe?

A little later in the poem, these haunting lines appear:

> I grow old . . . I grow old . . .
> I shall wear the bottoms of my trousers rolled.
>
> Shall I part my hair behind? Do I dare to eat a peach?
> I shall wear white flannel trousers, and walk upon the beach.

In South Florida, those trousers may be polyester, but I have seen them walk upon the beach. In South Florida, those trousers may have an elastic waistband and be part of a lady's three-piece pantsuit, but I have seen those trousers rolled. There in South Florida, I have seen them on tired women and on retired men. And I have seen old men with their hair parted just behind the ear with a few thin strands stretched across their pates. I have seen them—men and women—walk upon the beach and not dare to eat a peach. Or drink a cup of undecaffeinated coffee after 4:00 p.m., and I wonder—oh! I wonder—when does caution become reason? And I wonder, did any of these men, did any of these women, ever ask, "Do I dare disturb the universe?"

Who does ask, "Do I dare disturb the universe?"

And who does disturb the universe?

Kings did, and politicians do. The Wright brothers did, and NASA does. Martin Luther did, and John Paul does. Sigmund Freud did, and Dr. Ruth tries to. Rachel Carson did. Ralph Nader did. Betty Friedan did. Shakespeare did, and so did Michelangelo. Mozart did, and so did Picasso. Any creative act in some way disturbs the universe. A few great works change all the works that follow. No one who paints cannot not know the Sistine Ceiling, and no one who composes music cannot not know Beethoven—even if that person has never seen the Sistine Ceiling and even if that person has never heard Beethoven's Fifth. Michelangelo and Beethoven are there, somewhere; they tore up the ground they walked on, and they changed its contours, and even if we do not know whose footsteps we are following, we are walking over prepared soil.

We are beyond having a universe in which there is no Shakespeare.

If we are to discover what it takes to plow up the universe, let us examine the lives of some men who did. Let us track the lives of three men who disturbed the universe so profoundly that none of us in this room today can conceive of our universe without thinking of their disturbances. The three are men of science, and their work has dealt directly with our physical universe. All three are megamen of science, and they are—in order of appearance: Galileo, Newton, and Einstein. I have chosen them for two reasons: one, their disturbances are so profound that they are beyond value judgments. That is, we need not question the merit of what they have done as some might question the merit of the work of Sigmund Freud or Karl Marx or—in the Florida legislature at least—the work of Charles Darwin. And two, their accomplishments are so large that they allow us to examine in blow-up details that we might miss in lesser lives.

Let us go then, you and I, and examine the steps between a peach and the universe.

First Galileo.

Galileo was born in 1564, the year that Shakespeare was also born, and the year that Michelangelo died. When Galileo made himself a telescope—one which is on display to this very day in Florence—he discovered the moons of Jupiter. When he published his findings in a book to which he gave a beautiful title, *The Starry Messenger,* a Florentine astronomer proved in the following way that the satellites of Jupiter could not exist:

There are seven windows given to animals through which air is admitted to the tabernacle of the body . . .

**121**

What are these parts of the microcosmos? Two nostrils, two eyes, two ears and a mouth. So in the heavens, as in a macrocosmos, there are two favorable stars, two unpropitious, two luminaries and Mercury undecided and indifferent. From this and many other similarities in nature, such as the seven metals, et cetera, . . . we gather that the number of planets is necessarily seven. Moreover, these satellites of Jupiter are invisible to the naked eye and therefore would be useless and therefore do not exist. Besides the Jews and other ancient nations, as well as modern Europeans, have adopted the division of the week into seven days and have named them after the seven planets. Now if we increase the number of planets, this whole and beautiful system falls to the ground.

That was the mind-set that existed in Florence when Galileo lived there.

Galileo again turned his telescope toward the heavens and discovered something worse: Copernicus was right. The earth, by damn!, moved. The earth revolved around the sun, not vice versa.

And here Galileo's real troubles began.

The pope, Urban VIII, said that Galileo left no room for miracles. Monsignor Riccardi, the chief censor of the Roman Catholic church, said that Galileo was being blasphemous. He was correcting the Bible. Had not Solomon written:

. . . the Earth abideth for ever;
The Sun also ariseth,
and the Sun goeth down,
and hasteth to his place
where he ariseth . . .

And wasn't Solomon writing God's words—and Hemingway's future titles?

Galileo had an answer. He said, "The Bible shows the way

to go to Heaven, not the way the heavens go." But that answer was too wonderful, too witty, and it only made matters worse.

Remember, at this time the Catholic church was still reeling from the effects of the Reformation. It was the time of the Inquisition, and no one, especially the chief censor, could be accused of having a sense of humor in church matters.

But Galileo desperately wanted to publish, so he and the chief censor worked out a compromise. The chief censor said that Galileo could publish his findings if he agreed to write a preface in which he qualified his theories as "dreams, nullities, paralogisms, and chimera."

So, in 1632, *Dialogue on the Two Chief World Systems* was published. The two world systems were the Ptolemaic, that the sun revolved, and the Copernican, that the earth did. Galileo lived up to his part of the agreement, and he published his work with the disclaimer as approved by the censor.

But he did two other things wrong. First of all, he published in Italian, not in erudite Latin, and thus made his work accessible to all, and second, he wrote beautifully. He was a gifted writer of exposition, and then on top of all this, the quality of the research was so powerful that it proved Copernicanism beyond a doubt. It was like publishing a paper with a preface stating that the color red does not exist and then printing the entire text in red ink.

So Galileo was called before the Tribunal and forced to declare that he "abjured, cursed, and detested" his past errors.

The normal punishment for such heresy was imprisonment, but the pope commuted his sentence to house arrest on the condition that Galileo "repeat once a week the seven penitential psalms"–and Galileo did–and never talk to any Protestants–and Galileo did not.

And that is what happened to you in the year 1633 if you dared to disturb the universe.

But was it really disturbing the universe that mattered so much? Was it really troubles with the universe that caused such profound troubles for the man Galileo?

Please remember that he was born in the same year that Shakespeare was. We all know that in 1633, when Galileo got into trouble, England had been Protestant for a hundred years. But Galileo wanted to publish in his neighborhood, not Shakespeare's. If he had chosen to publish in a country just a little farther north, say Germany or Holland, he would have met with far fewer problems. Even Venice, an Italian city but one with a freer and looser society, would never have troubled him the way his own neighborhood did. For between a peach and the universe, there is the neighborhood, and those who dare disturb the universe must first have the courage to dare disturb the neighborhood.

It takes more courage to disturb the neighborhood than it takes to disturb the universe. And the price is often higher.

So, between a peach and the universe, we have the lesson of Galileo—that it takes more courage to disturb the neighborhood than it does to disturb the universe.

—✦—

In the very year that Galileo died, Isaac Newton was born into Protestant England, where the neighborhood was friendly to science. It is here, in the person of Newton, that Galileo's work would be extended, and it is from the person of Isaac Newton that we can see what, besides daring to disturb the neighborhood, it takes to disturb the universe.

The year in which Newton was born was important, not only because his work started where Galileo's left off— it did—but also because, having been born in 1642 meant that in 1665, Newton was ready to start graduate school at Cambridge University, and that year is significant because

1665 was a plague year. By August of 1665, one-tenth of the population of London had died of the plague, so in September Cambridge called off all its classes. School was closed; its students were sent home. Isaac Newton among them.

Home to Isaac Newton was a small stone house in Woolsthorpe, where his mother lived and where it is supposed there was an apple tree. Newton was devoted to his mother, and she to him, but there was no one in Woolsthorpe with whom he could discuss his intellectual achievements.

There, in those two plague years, 1665 and 1666, Newton formulated his three great laws of motion: inertia, gravitational attraction, and action-reaction; developed the laws of pendulum motion; worked out the inverse square law; proved Kepler's laws of planetary motion; developed the mathematical treatment of wave motion; worked out the main irregularities of the moon's motion; explained the tides; showed that comets are members of the solar system and that the density of the earth is between five and six times that of water, and figured out the precession of the equinoxes. He also conducted experiments that led to important discoveries about the refraction of light and the nature of color.

Not bad. But wait, there's more.

As a mathematical tool to help himself solve the problems he was working on, Newton invented differential and integral calculus. He called his invention *fluxions*.

He invented something else as a tool. Just as Galileo was witty, Newton was handy. When he was studying light, he ground his own prisms, and when he was studying the stars, he invented the reflecting telescope. The reflecting telescope—and Newton himself along with it—came to the attention of the Royal Society of London for the Promotion of Natural Knowledge, known as the Royal Society, and it was at the urging of its president that in 1687, his major work,

*The Principia,* was published. The *People* magazine part of me makes me need to tell you that the president of the Royal Society at that time was none other than Samuel Pepys, the diarist, and the book itself was financed by Edmond Halley of Halley's comet fame. The travel guide part of me makes me need to tell you that Newton's telescope is on display at the Royal Observatory in Greenwich.

Most of us would have been proud to have claimed the invention of the reflecting telescope or the invention of calculus in those two plague years. I, for one, would have considered it an accomplishment to have mastered the use of calculus in two years. I certainly didn't do it in two semesters at college.

There is an awful lot about Sir Isaac Newton that *People* magazine could have feasted upon. He was petty and mean, wise and generous, a mystic and a civil servant, but the aspect that I want now to emphasize, the aspect that I think all who are interested in disturbing the universe must know about, is his ability to profitably survive a plague year. I don't mean physical ability.

I mean mental ability.

I mean mental agility.

I mean that those who would disturb the universe have a need for solitude. And that, I think, is the second step between a peach and the universe: the ability to be alone profitably—to enjoy solitude with vigor.

—✦—

Like Newton, Einstein was isolated from other physicists at the time he published his first paper on relativity. He was working as a technical expert third class in the patent office of Bern, Switzerland.

And like Galileo, Einstein also disturbed his neighborhood.

In 1933 Philipp Lenard, a 1905 recipient of the Nobel Prize, wrote in the Nazi paper:

The most important example of the dangerous influence of Jewish circles on the study of nature has been provided by Herr Einstein with his mathematically botched theories consisting of some ancient knowledge and a few arbitrary additions . . . Even scientists who have otherwise done solid work . . . allowed the relativity theory to get a foothold in Germany because they did not see . . . how wrong it is . . . to regard this Jew as a good German.

Later in a speech, Lenard said:

"We must recognize that it is unworthy of a German to be the intellectual follower of a Jew. Natural science . . . is of completely Aryan origin, and Germans must today also find their own way out into the unknown. *Heil Hitler."*

By 1933 Einstein had disturbed his neighborhood to the point of personal danger, so he left his native Germany and moved to Princeton. Shortly after moving there he wrote to a friend:

Princeton is a wonderful little spot, a quaint and ceremonious village of puny demigods on stilts. Yet by ignoring certain social conventions I have been able to create for myself an atmosphere conducive to study and free of distraction. Here the people who compose what is called "society" enjoy even less freedom than their counterparts in Europe. Yet, they seem unaware of this restriction, since their way of life tends to inhibit personality development from childhood.

In that single statement Einstein summarizes how a need for solitude and the courage to disturb the neighborhood, points one and two between a peach and the universe, feed each other.

Do I dare ignore the neighborhood? And do I dare demand solitude?

It is Einstein who directly reveals the third ingredient that is necessary if a person dares to disturb the universe. He said, "When I examine myself and my methods of thought, I come to the conclusion that the gift of fantasy has meant more to me than my talent for absorbing positive knowledge."

Einstein made that comment in a conversation with Janos Plesch about the similarities between writing fiction and working mathematics. And thus, this man of genius kindly makes a perfect transition for me, speaking about the creative process, applied—as I know it best—to writing fiction. For the third ingredient between a peach and the universe is the gift of fantasy.

As a writer of novels for middle-aged children, kids between the ages of eight and twelve, I have been concerned with each of these steps between a peach and the universe, for neighborhoods, solitude, and fantasy are not only what it takes to make me write, but they are also what I write about, for neighborhoods, solitude, and fantasy are the concerns of children between the ages of eight and twelve.

Let me start with fantasy.

Even if you are writer of realistic fiction for children, fantasy enters into the *process* of writing. The writing itself is the result of fantasy. I tell my children when they ask that when I sit down to write, I start the movie in my head.

But fantasy often enters into the actual story I am telling. From my very first book, *Jennifer, Hecate, Macbeth, William McKinley and Me, Elizabeth*, there has been at least one element of "let's pretend" in each of my books. *Up From Jericho Tel* begins:

There was a time when I was eleven years old—
between the start of a new school year and Mid-

winter's Night—when I was invisible. I was never invisible for long, and I always returned to plain sight, but all my life has been affected by the people I met and the time I spent in a world where I could see and not be seen.

I indulged a favorite fantasy, being invisible, when I wrote that book, but beyond that, I hope I give my readers a sense of suspending disbelief, a sense of fantasy.

Every now and then I get a letter that tells me I have done that. Here's one such letter. It is dated September 18, 1970.

> Dear Mrs. Konigsburg,
> My name is Lorraine Piotrowski, and I am 11 years old. (I think that's a sensible age, don't you?) I live in Ontario and have read your books called: About the B'nai Bagels and From the Mixed-up Files of Mrs. Basil E. Frankweiler. I thought both of them were delicious, and I ate them up in my mind, and now and then the taste comes back to me . . .

When I get a letter like that, I know that even the most realistic fiction not only fills a need for fantasy in the reader but also feeds solitude. As Lorraine Piotrowski puts it, "I ate them up in my mind, and now and then the taste comes back to me." Fiction makes solitude rich. Fiction makes solitude taste good.

The need for solitude has also been one of the concerns about which I write. It was a concern with the need of a suburban child to have time alone that most directly prompted my writing *About the B'nai Bagels,* one of the books that Lorraine Piotrowski mentioned. *About the B'nai Bagels* is the story of a young boy, Mark Setzer, who is middle-class suburban and whose time not spent at school is spent preparing for his Bar Mitzvah or at Little League. When his mother becomes manager of his Little League team, even his play time is invaded, and when she appoints his big brother Spencer as his coach, poor Mark cannot escape his family at all. I think we would say that his family had invaded his space.

I close that book with my young hero, Mark Setzer, solving a moral dilemma, having his Bar Mitzvah, and then this last paragraph. Mark is speaking:

> According to Hebrew Law, now I am a man. That is, I can participate fully in all religious services. But I figure that you don't become a man overnight. Because it is a becoming, becoming more yourself, your own kind of tone deaf, center-fielder, son, brother, friend, Bagel. And only some of it happens on official time plus family time. A lot of it happens being alone. And it doesn't happen overnight. Sometimes it takes a guy a whole Little League season.

Even if you appreciate solitude, as Mark Setzer comes to, it is not always easy to come by.

The need for solitude gets no respect. Especially if you are a woman experiencing that need.

An American woman.

An American suburban woman.

A married American suburban woman.

A married American suburban woman with children . . . who works.

Do you ever wonder—as I do—where it is written that the wife is instantly available to find the flat-headed screwdriver even if she doesn't even know what one is? Do you ever believe—as I do—that children come with a gene that says it is mothers and not fathers who are instantly interruptible to explain where she put the skateboard, the hair dryer, and the WD-40 even if she has never used them? Do you ever think—as I do—that a plague year would be welcome if it meant a year without a supper-time phone call from the aluminum siding salesperson?

Aside from these interruptions, there are forces acting on

women over which they have no control. I think of a study done several years ago in Denver. Within a year of living together, nurses in a dormitory had all their menstrual cycles fall to within a few days of one another even though, initially, their periods had been weeks apart. When I mentioned the remarkable implications of this to a young friend who was in college, living in a coed dormitory, she said, "That's strange; the same thing happened to me and my friends."

I don't know if it also happened when I lived in a college dormitory because I went to college in an era when no one ever dreamed that tampon commercials would appear on TV, and cigarette commercials would not. Periods were mentioned in public only as the full stop at the end of a sentence. But do you wonder—as I do—if women were not meant to have solitude but were meant to be part of a pack for some communal, territorial, arena-stomping male selection process?

But if given a choice, I would rather have an unsatisfied need for solitude than have no need for it at all. Einstein once said, "Perhaps, some day solitude will come to be properly recognized and appreciated as the teacher of personality. The Orientals have long known this. The individual who has experienced solitude will not easily become a victim of mass suggestion." The art of being alone with vigor is a talent. Like all talent, it must be developed, and if the Orientals have developed it more, some cultures develop it less.

That this is so became apparent to me in 1981 when I was in Texas for a speaking engagement at Southwest Texas State University. On the evening before my lecture, my host was a retired navy man who was seriously indulging his love of history, particularly Texas history. There is no state's history more intertwined with Mexico than that of Texas, and he had a profound interest in both. He had been born in the Midwest but grew up in Mexico. His wife referred to him as her American-Mexican husband. Long after the evening was mellow, he asked me a question that I could not answer then and have difficulty answering now.

His question was this: Why since there has developed a broad acceptance of minority cultures in the United States, why since there has developed a body of children's literature produced by Asian-Americans and African-Americans, why has there been no work, let alone a body of work, produced by Mexican-Americans? There are books about them, but there are no books by them.

I pleaded with him that although I write books for children, I am not and never have claimed to be an authority on them. But when I asked an authority, she came up with one book: Aurora Labastida wrote the text for the picture book *Nine Days to Christmas,* published in 1959.

I continued to give a lot of thought to his question. I asked teachers and counselors who worked in Mexican-American neighborhoods, and they reported that life in the barrio represents a kind of togetherness that is almost unknown on the outside. Living is done in groups. Women visit while shopping, watching television, going to the launderette, eating. Is it possible that the child never has a chance to develop a talent for being alone? Is it possible that the barrio is protection but is also a prison? Is it as sweet as a marshmallow and just as hard to punch out of?

How can a person disturb the neighborhood if a person never learns to be solitary? How can a culture produce disturbers of the universe if it never unleashes its members from the neighborhood? There must be solitude, and there must be something to feed that solitude, and I believe that books should. Certainly books are a more alone—a more one-to-one—activity than television.

Thus, books enrich fantasy, and books enrich solitude. But by one of those wonderful organic paradoxes, it is equally true that fantasy and solitude enrich books and make possible the writing of them.

Writers need to dream, and writers need to be alone. For I am convinced there can be no creative process without fantasy and without solitude. And I am equally convinced that a writer, even if he is not writing about the earth circling the sun, even if he is writing fiction, must have the courage to disturb the neighborhood. Thomas Wolfe could not go home to Asheville again after writing *Look Homeward, Angel.* I know people in New Jersey who still will not speak to Philip Roth, and I know a town in Vermont where a Nobel Laureate lived because he found that it was easier to disturb Mother Nature than to disturb Mother Russia. Novelist Salman Rushdie has to keep his current neighborhood a secret because he disturbed his old one.

As a writer of fiction for middle-aged children, I have often addressed the need to disturb the neighborhood. There is no time in a child's life when the question, Do I dare disturb the neighborhood? is more pressing than when he is in grades five through eight, for that is the time when children are being pulled by their peers on the one hand and by their core selves on the other.

To illustrate my concern with gathering the courage it takes to disturb the neighborhood, I would like to present excerpts from a story called "With Bert and Ray" from my collection of short stories called *Throwing Shadows.* William is telling the story. It begins:

> If I have to start at the beginning of things, I guess I would have to start with Pa. Or the end of Pa, I should say. I had long ago heard the expression of someone being *dead drunk.* Well, that was Pa. Or the end of Pa. He died dead drunk when I was six, and that was as many years ago. Half my life ago. For a long time before he died, he couldn't get anyone to sell him any more insurance, and I can't say that I blame them. Anyway, the little bit he did have, didn't hardly pay for his funeral, and the little bit that Ma

got from Social Security didn't hardly carry us from one month to the next.

So what Ma did, after Pa had been dead for three years, and we had some powerful dentist bills mounted up, was to sell off all his stuff. Wasn't any of it she wanted anyways . . . hunting guns and duck decoys and all the issues of *National Geographic* back to when it was started.

Two of the people who came to the sale were Bert and Ray, this couple who have an antique store over in the section of town called Huntington. Bert and Ray were kinda thrilled about the duck decoys and the price Ma had put on them. They sure did tuck them decoys under their arms real quick and paid Ma exactly what she asked for them and gave her a card, saying that she should please to call them whenever she did another house sale. Ma took the card and said that she sure would call them if she ever did another. I was speculating about what Ma could sell until I realized that Ma is just a timid soul who says "scuse me" to the chiffonier when she bumps into it.

Soon William and his mother are over in the Huntington section of town for their dental appointments, and, as they are waiting for the bus, William notices that they are right at Bert and Ray's shop. William takes the initiative and makes his mother pay them a visit. Shortly afterward, William's mother gets a call from Ray asking her if she would like to handle a house sale for them.

Ma said sure she'd like to help them, not even knowing what was in it for her, but she wanted to thank them for having her and me to tea. She asked Ray if I, William, could help, too. I guess she figured that I ought to since I had had some tea, too, and Ray told her yes, that certainly William could help.

The sale turned out real good. We cleared out that whole houseful of stuff and made two hundred forty-three dollars and thirty-eight cents for our work, and that was the start of our career managing house sales.

Business is good, and William and his mother begin upgrading their household by buying things—at fair market value—from their estate sales, and Bert and Ray begin upgrading their business by traveling to far places to buy fancier antiques. William continues his story:

Ma and me came to see how the hardest part about antiques is finding them and buying them at a good price. Selling them is pretty easy except for some things and those things aren't necessarily the ugliest. Sometimes ugly sells real good. It depends on the style of ugly. Ma had gathered together a little library of books, but she didn't never do the pricing if Bert and Ray were around and if they showed even by a quick look in their eyes that they wanted to keep in practice. Ma always let them because she told me she didn't want to hurt their feelings none, and she didn't want to give them the idea that she had forgot from whence all her new career had sprung.

One day when Ma and me were invited over to Bert and Ray's for tea, they had just come back from a buying trip up to Kentucky and some other horse country . . . when Ma spotted this piece of furniture leaning by the wall that leads to their parlor . . . and Ma went on over to it and studied on it a while and said, "I just love your panetière, Bert. Wherever did you find it?"

"Panetière?" Bert said. "What panetière?"

"That there cupboard," Ma said, pointing to the piece of furniture leaning against the parlor wall.

"This'n," I said. "Ma called it a panetière."

Then Ma looked at the ticket and said, "I see that y'all made a good buy. A right good buy."

Ray came in from the kitchen just then, and Bert

said to him, "It seems to me that we made a good buy on our panetière, Ray."

And Ray said, "Our what?"

"Your panetière right there," I said, pointing to that same cupboard leaning against the parlor wall.

Ray got real upset. I know he did. So did Bert. They smiled, both of them did, but I could tell . . . I peeked back in the door after we left, and I saw them pulling the tag off of that there panetière, which they didn't even know they had until Ma called it to their attention.

Next week Ma had Bert and Ray over to supper, and Ray announced, "Bert and I sold our panetière to Mrs. Sinclair. She's doing everything in French, and we called her and told her that we had an authentic eighteenth century bread cupboard, and she didn't even know it was a panetière until we told her. She bought it like that," he said, snapping his fingers.

"Fancy that," I said, "a genuine eighteenth century panetière, and Mrs. Sinclair didn't even know it."

Bert said, "Well some of these people who have big houses need to be educated in good taste."

Ma just smiled and told them how glad she was that they had turned a nice profit.

William and Ma get a call to handle the Birchfield estate, where they find a Chinese silk screen. No one buys it at the sale, and Bert and Ray even make fun of it, saying that it's a piece of junk. William's mother, convinced that it is something fine, buys it from the estate for $125 and takes it home and studies it. She becomes increasingly convinced that it is something special. William takes Polaroid pictures of it and during his class trip to Washington, D.C., he makes his way to the Freer Gallery, where they indicate some interest; so when school is out, William and Ma load the screen into their station wagon and go with it to the Freer. Her asking price is twenty thousand dollars. William finishes telling the story.

When we'd been back home eight days, we got a telegram from the museum saying the committee had voted to purchase the screen. I called up the newspaper and told them, and a writer from the newspaper came on over to the house and listened to Ma's story and published two of my Polaroids besides, not even complaining that they were a little out of focus or that they had fingerprints on them in the wrong places.

We must have got a hundred phone calls the day the story come out in the paper. I told Ma that what I couldn't understand was why Bert and Ray hadn't called us up to congratulate us. A lot of other dealers had. Ma said that she understood why they had not, and she was feeling pretty sad about it.

I asked Ma if she thought that they was jealous about the money. Ma said that the money was just a little bit of it. "What do you suppose is the big part of it then, Ma?" I asked.

"It's hard for me to know the words for saying it, William," she said. "I know what it is that's bothering them. It's the same thing that bothered them about the panetière, but I don't know the psychological words for it."

Bert and Ray finally called the next day, and I heard Ma say, "It seems like I got took pretty good, Bert. I found out that that there screen I sold to the museum for twenty thousand dollars was really worth twenty-five. Guess I just still got a lot to learn."

Well, that was it.

Bert and Ray come on over to the house that night and teased Ma about how she got took and Ma just laughed at herself right along with them.

Well, that was it.

Bert and Ray just couldn't stand being beat out by Ma, who had been their student just a few years ago. Bert and Ray couldn't stand it that Ma already knowed more about antiques than they did, not only because she studies on them but also because she got all these delicate feelings about things that you can't hardly help but notice when you watch her looking at something or touching it so gentle.

But Ma's been so wore down by everything, including living all them years with Pa, that she figures won't nobody love her if she shows that she knows one thing more than they do.

But I look back on how good she stuck by her guns with that screen, and I figure that if she can stand by her guns with strangers, she soon will be able to with people who have us over to tea. And I figure that I got six more years before I finish school and have to go off and leave her, and I'm going to work on her. I pushed her up them steps to Huntington Antiques, and I got her to go to that museum, and I'm sure that I can help her to find out how being grateful to Bert and Ray is something she should always be, but outgrown them is something she already is. By the time I leave home, she's going to be ready to face that fact and live with it. She'll need it, being's she won't have me around to push her here and there any more.

—✛—

This story was sparked from my reading an account of how in 1963 the Metropolitan Museum of Art acquired its polychrome statue of St. John the Baptist by the Spanish master, Juan Martínez Montañes. It is a beauty. I recommend that the next time you visit the Metropolitan Museum of Art you seek out the majestic statue that Mildred Centers bought for sixty-five dollars and sold to the museum for eighteen thousand dollars.

Mildred Centers lives in Jacksonville, Florida.

So you see, my immediate neighborhood is in the background of this story about disturbing the neighborhood . . . step one between a peach and the universe.

—✦—

Before my time to ask, Do I dare to eat a peach? I want to
ask, Do I dare to dream? Do I dare enjoy my solitude? Do I
dare disturb the neighborhood?

And
If I do,
And if I dare,
I may write a book about someone who does.
Or
I may write a book that does.
Or
I may disturb the universe.

# Winding up the 80s

Since I wrote "Between a Peach and the Universe" the number of Mexican-American books by Mexican-American authors has grown. I do not know how many. I simply know there are more.

The number of children's books written by Chinese-Americans and Japanese-Americans has grown, too. So have those by Hmong-Americans, Native American-Americans, and Tex-Mex-Americans. I do not know how many. I simply know there are more, for multiculturalism is the latest trend in the field of children's literature.

Children love to read about themselves. In my Newbery address, I said that reading about families such as those depicted in *Mary Poppins* and *The Secret Garden* made me think "that they were the norm and that the way I lived was sub-normal, waiting for normal." When I was a child, it would have been wonderful to read about a Jewish girl living in a small mill town with a father who worked long hours and a mother who "helped out in the store." How I would have loved to see my father's rich Hungarian accent translated into print. It would, as I have said, have added a dimension to reality. (Hungarians put the accent on the first syllable of words. Thus, my father spoke of *lapp*-ils for lapels.

**140**

You can guess the correct pronunciation of our family name: Lobl.)

Farrell, Pennsylvania, where I graduated from high school, had as its motto, An Industrial City of Friendly People. If we were writing that motto today, it would be called An Industrial City of Friendly Ethnic People. But we didn't know we were ethnic. We were a city of 12,500 people living in mixed neighborhoods where no one tried to keep up with the Joneses because, as I have said, there was no one named Jones in my class.

Within its population of 12,500, Farrell had the following social clubs: Polish, Bulgarian, Serbian, Romanian, Slovenian, Hungarian, Italian, Carpo-Russ, German as well as Saxon, Greek as well as Macedonian, a Young Men's Hebrew Association, the Twin City Elks, which was all black, and three Croatian Homes. Members of the club met with a level of social comfort in the alien New World. It was in the privacy of these clubs that the Croats, the Serbs, the Saxons, et cetera, kept alive their traditions and language and memories of the old country while their children were becoming Americans. Each of us children of immigrants was free to keep the customs of our parents or modify them or abandon them. Sometimes we mixed; sometimes we matched. The Zahariou girls and Achilles Mouganis studied Greek after school just as the Jewish kids studied Hebrew after school. The kids whose parents belonged to the Macedonian Club as well as the ones whose parents belonged to the Greek Club all became Americans. As did I.

Now, in the interest of multiculturalism, children's books are being asked to do for the new generation of immigrants what ethnic social clubs once did for my parents'. They are being asked to make a record, and that is fine. They are being asked to give comfort, recognition, and respect, and that is fine, too. But I have some concerns about this latest trend in children's literature.

What, you may ask, are the concerns of a woman who began this series of speeches bleating about how "the writing of it [the Radasevitches and the Gabellas] makes normal of it." Does she want to pull up the ladder after having her turn?

No, I do not want to pull up the ladder, and no, I don't want to stop minorities from seeing themselves in books.

But I am concerned that books written in response to a trend–particularly a trend in subject matter–result in proliferation, not growth.

Two excerpts from an article in the September 9, 1991, issue of *Newsweek* magazine under the heading It's a Not So Small World, subheading *Multiculturalism Is Broadening the Horizons of Children's Literature,* help to illustrate my concerns:

> One of the people most responsible for the high standards of these [multicultural] books is Harriet Rohmer, founder of Children's Book Press in San Francisco . . . For "The Invisible Hunters" ($12.95), a Miskito Indian folk tale about the first contact of an isolated tribe with the outside world, Rohmer herself tracked down fragments of the story all over Nicaragua; she got a piece of it in one village, another piece down the road, until she could put it all together.

Are these needle biopsies–placing smaller and smaller slivers of civilization under the microscope–discovering differences or creating them?

> All of [Rohmer's] books are multicultural, and every story is told (often bilingually) by an author who shares the story's culture. Blia Xiong is from Laos, and her story, "Nine-in-One Grr! Grr!" ($12.95) is about the Hmong tribe. Artist Carmen Lomas Garza's "Family Pictures" ($13.95) depicts her own Mexican-American childhood in south Texas . . . Rohmer's insistence on authentic ethnic storytellers was unique when she began publishing. Now it is becoming commonplace.

Who decides who is an authentic ethnic storyteller? In 1971 Gail Haley won a Caldecott Medal for *A Story A Story,* an African folktale, and in 1975 Jean Craighead George won the Newbery Medal for *Julie of the Wolves,* the story of an Inuit girl; would that be possible in 1994?

Can only the Hmong write Hmong books?

Is *The Invisible Hunters* as told by Harriet Rohmer more authentic? more ethnic? than *Julie of the Wolves* as written by Jean Craighead George?

Tolstoy was not a woman when he wrote *Anna Karenina* and William Styron was neither a mother nor a concentration-camp survivor when he wrote *Sophie's Choice.*

I am a Jewish-American female. Of Hungarian descent. From a small town. I am a middle-child, small-town, Jewish-American female of Hungarian descent. But that is not all that I am. I am also overweight, prone to headaches, and a klutz. Everything that I write may run through that filter, but filters are not made of the materials they are meant to distill. Just because Baryshnikov has not asked me to dance doesn't mean I don't know it will be wonderful when he does.

I am more than what I was, more than what I am, and part of the reason that I am is because I have learned to wear many masks. I have been allowed to wear many masks because Western civilization–flawed though it may be–has given me the privacy and privilege to do so.

In years to come, will today's new immigrants ask the question: Must the Hmong write *only* Hmong books? I hope they ask; I also hope they won't have to.

Because I so profoundly believe that books must come from the hearts and minds of writers, because of the nature of writers and the written, because I say, "Glory be to God for dappled things," because I believe that the whole of *Rashomon* is a single truth, because I believe there is a distinction between truth and accuracy, I also don't believe that wolves must write wolf books.

# 8. The Mask Beneath the Face

My mother used to say, "If you really want to know someone, marry him or play cards with him." My mother would say that; she lived in a time when a lot of people believed that the only way nice women really got to know a member of the opposite sex was to marry him, and, besides, she was a terrific poker player. In these modern times when a person does not have to marry someone to know him, and the fine art of poker playing has moved out of the family living room and into the casinos of Atlantic City and Las Vegas, I would like to add that if you really want to know someone, take him to Mardi Gras.

Going to Mardi Gras had long been an item on my lifetime checklist of things to do before I die. Now that I've been, I can tell you that there are three things wrong with it. One, it is crowded. Two, it is gaudy. And three, it is vulgar. On the other hand, Mardi Gras has three things to recommend it. One, it is crowded. Two, it is gaudy. And three, it is vulgar.

If you want clean and orderly, go to Disney World. If you want vulgarity that is considered to be good taste, go to Williamsburg, Virginia. Mardi Gras, like the city that hosts it, has spontaneity and squalor and charm. There is something authentic about Mardi Gras in New Orleans, and despite its exaggerations of dress and deportment–perhaps, because of them–a person senses she'll find some truth there in the ungentrified French Quarter.

Throughout the French Quarter during Mardi Gras, people wore outfits that were outrageous and funny. They wore tinsel wigs and had their faces painted. Men dressed as women; women dressed as men. The fine lines that separate costume from dress, male from female, good taste from bad, disappeared.

Sometimes under a layer of face paint or beneath a feathered mask, the last boundary, that between acceptable and unacceptable social behavior, also disappeared. Young women wearing masks and others with painted faces leaned over balconies and pulled down their panties or pulled up their T-shirts, exposing that–or those–which are normally hidden.

Strangely enough, it was the masks that seemed to me to be the most revealing. The masks held the key to the truth that I sensed there. Then the question became: Were people behind the masks exhibiting the persona of the mask they had assumed or were they showing their true character? Did the masks allow them to conceal their true selves? Or reveal them?

Were the false faces ones they could assume? Or were they ones they could hide behind?

Were they disguise?

Or were they protection?

I arrived home wondering about the behavior behind the masks of Mardi Gras and asked my husband, the psychologist, Dr. David Konigsburg, "Do you think wearing a mask allows a person to be someone else, or do you think that a mask allows a person to be that which he really is?" And my husband, the psychologist, Dr. David Konigsburg, answered, "Yes."

Before I could express my annoyance, he pointed out that in my work, I had said, yes, they reveal as well as yes, they conceal. He also mentioned that my fascination with masks was nothing new. It had started with my very first book. With the very first scene of my very first book. He was right, of course. Allow me, please, to demonstrate.

Elizabeth, who is ten, begins her story (and my career as a writer) in *Jennifer, Hecate, Macbeth, William McKinley and Me, Elizabeth* as follows:

> I first met Jennifer on my way to school. It was Halloween, and she was sitting in a tree . . . I was dressed as a Pilgrim . . . I had my head way back and was watching the leaves when I first saw Jennifer up in the tree . . . She was sitting on one of the lower branches . . . swinging her feet . . . [She was wearing] real Pilgrim shoes made of buckles and cracked old leather. The heel part flapped up and down because the shoes were so big that only the toe part could stay attached . . .
> "You're going to lose that shoe," I said.
> The first thing Jennifer said to me was, "Witches never lose anything."
> "But you're not a witch," I said. "You're a Pilgrim, and look, so am I."
> "I won't argue with you," she said. "Witches convince; they never argue. But I'll tell you this much. Real witches are Pilgrims, and just because I don't have on a silly black costume and carry a silly broom and wear a silly black hat, doesn't mean that I'm not a witch. I'm a witch all the time and not just on Halloween."

When they go trick-or-treating later that evening, Elizabeth asks Jennifer why she isn't wearing a mask.

> She answered that one disguise was enough. She told me that all year long she was a witch, disguised as a perfectly normal girl; on Halloween she became undisguised.

E.L. Konigsburg

So in my first book, Jennifer decides that masks make you somebody you aren't.

But in a later book, Sabrina in *Journey to an 800 Number* thinks just the opposite. Maximilian, the narrator and hero of this story, meets Sabrina, a girl about his age who collects newspaper articles about freaks. Max expresses some impatience with her fascination, and Sabrina replies:

> "Maximilian, what you don't seem to understand is that once you're a freak, a born one or a man-made one, anything you do that's normal becomes freakish."
>
> "By your logic, then, anything freakish that a freak does is normal."
>
> "Sure. Now, you take David."
>
> "I know a lot of Davids. Which David?"
>
> "The boy in the bubble in Houston. His name is David. He has something wrong with him so that his body cannot fight germs, so he lives in a room-sized container where air is pumped in and germs are kept out. If you were to sneeze at David, you could kill him. He's nine years old now, and the only reason he has reached the age of nine is that he's never tried to be normal. He never tried to be anything but a freak."
>
> "But Renee was not born defective. She's the victim of an accident. She can still live a normal life."
>
> "I wouldn't call it normal."
>
> "She can overcome what happened to her."
>
> "Overcoming is not normal. Overcoming means always having to do that plus whatever else she wants to do. It's like she will always have to put something on before she puts on her clothes . . . It's like putting on a suit of armor before you put on your clothes. Everything you wear takes the shape of the armor."
>
> "I'd say that makes it basically hard to relax."
>
> "And to pretend."
>
> "Why would anyone want to pretend?"
>
> "Everyone wants to pretend sometime. Needs to. But freaks . . . cannot live with disguises. Only nor-

**147**

mal people like you and me and Lilly and Woody
have any choice about whether or not we want to
present ourselves or present a disguise."

On February 7, 1984, David, the boy in the bubble, was
allowed to touch the world unprotected. He crawled out of
his bubble and into a hospital room specially equipped to
keep the air as sterile as possible. He was kissed by his mother for the first time, gave his father and sister hugs, sat in a
chair, and heard sounds clearly instead of through plastic.
David died on February 22, 1984. He was twelve.

Maybe Sabrina is right, and there are times when the only
way you can be yourself is to hide behind a mask. But maybe
Jennifer is also right: wearing a mask allows you to pretend, to
become someone else. And maybe that is a privilege that only
normal people have, while those people who are not normal
wear a mask so that they can be the person they really are. Yes
may, after all, be the correct answer to both of those questions.

Masks have a place in my latest novel as well as my first,
and in some form they are featured in works in between; for
those of us who write fiction, it is Fat Tuesday whenever we
go to work, for we use our characters as masks. Wearing
masks is what writers do, and the masks that one assumes as
a writer serve the same purpose as those at Mardi Gras: they
reveal; they conceal; they exaggerate, and they do it all for
the sake of getting at some truth that is often seen but not
fully understood.

The history of a masked storyteller is older than writing
itself. Long ago, a priest or a shaman donned the mask of an
animal whose spirit he wanted to assume. While wearing an
appropriate animal mask, he danced and sang to an assembly
of tribesmen, relating the courage of the lion, the swiftness
of the eagle, the cunning of the wolf. These animals were
their tribal totems, their ancestral spirits. Even today we celebrate the vestiges of these totem masks when we say "Go

Gators" or when we cheer the Panthers of Pittsburgh, the Nittany Lions or those of Detroit, or the Tigers of LSU or Clemson or Princeton or Detroit.

The Greeks introduced masks into literature through the theater. In ancient Greece, the worship of Dionysus, god of fecundity and the harvest, evolved from first impersonating the deity by donning goat skins to finally making masks. The masked man spoke in the first person, assuming the persona of the god, and the art of drama was born.

Tellers of folktales did as the shaman did and as the performers in Greek theater. Tellers of folktales abstract the characteristics of an animal and form them into stories, but the masks now are words, and there is often a plot to the tale.

Let me show you four wolf masks, four masks that reveal the wolf. The first is a severe, uncompromising mask from the tales of the Brothers Grimm.

> Little Red Riding Hood went up to the bed and drew back the curtains; there lay the grandmother with her cap pulled over her eyes so that she looked very odd.
> "O grandmother, what large ears you have got!"
> "The better to hear with."
> "O grandmother, what great eyes you have got!"
> "The better to see with."
> "O grandmother, what large hands you have got!"
> "The better to take hold of you with."
> "But grandmother, what a terrible large mouth you have got!"
> "The better to devour you!" And no sooner had the wolf said it than he made one bound from the bed, and swallowed up poor Little Red Riding Hood.
> Then the wolf, having satisfied his hunger, lay down again in the bed, went to sleep, and began to snore loudly.

Here we have the wolf in drag, which would seem to be the converse of the man in the wolf mask, but isn't it still the shaman striking fear and respect into tender hearts? Isn't it still the wolf doing and the wolf saying what the man in a wolf mask believes a wolf would say and do? The story of Little Red Riding Hood is fearsome and uncompromising and altogether suitable for its time and altogether suitable for preschoolers, who are equally fearsome and uncompromising.

In time the wolf masks of children's tales grow more sophisticated. In a later story, they are just as feared, but they do not dress up, and they do not speak. Listen to Laura Ingalls Wilder tell about wolves outside the door of her *Little House in the Big Woods:*

> At night, when Laura lay awake in the trundle bed, she listened and could not hear anything at all but the sound of the trees whispering together. Sometimes, far away in the night, a wolf howled. Then he came nearer and howled again.
>
> It was a scary sound. Laura knew that wolves would eat little girls. But she was safe inside the solid log walls. Her father's gun hung over the door and good old Jack, the brindle bull dog, lay on guard before it. Her father would say, "Go to sleep, Laura. Jack won't let the wolves in." So Laura snuggled under the covers of the trundle bed, close beside Mary, and went to sleep.

In this story of frontier life in the late nineteenth century there is a wall between man and the wolf. No one wants to acquire his attributes. There is no Go Wolfpack here. The wolf at the door was not to be admired but to be feared.

A generation later, fear still features in a portrait of a wolf. But it is fear mingled with admiration. Jack London donned the mask of the heroic lead dog, Buck, to get under the mask of the wolf. This part of the story comes toward the end, when Buck discovers that the master who saved his life and whom he loved above all others is dead, and he answers *The Call of the Wild.*

John Thornton was dead. The last tie was broken. Man and the claims of man no longer bound him. . . . [T]he wolf pack had at last crossed over from the land of streams and timber and invaded Buck's valley. Into the clearing where the moonlight streamed, they poured in a silvery flood; and in the centre of the clearing stood Buck, motionless as a statue, waiting their coming. They were awed, so still and large he stood, and a moment's pause fell, till the boldest one leaped straight for him. Like a flash Buck struck, breaking the neck. Then he stood, without movement, as before, the stricken wolf rolling in agony behind him. Three others tried it in sharp succession; and one after the other they drew back, streaming blood from slashed throats or shoulders . . . Pivoting on his hind legs, and snapping and gashing, [Buck] was everywhere at once . . . [A]t the end of half an hour the wolves drew back discomfited. The tongues of all were out and lolling, the white fangs showing cruelly white in the moonlight . . . One wolf, long and lean and gray, advanced cautiously, in a friendly manner . . . He was whining softly, and, as Buck whined, they touched noses.

Then an old wolf, gaunt and battle-scarred, came forward. Buck writhed his lips into the preliminary of a snarl, but sniffed noses with him. Whereupon the old wolf sat down, pointed nose at the moon, and broke out the long wolf howl. The others sat down and howled. And now the call came to Buck in unmistakable accents. He, too, sat down and howled . . .

Jack London peeks under the mask of the wolf and finds that all wolves are not alike; they may be killers, but they are selective. Fear is mixed with admiration, not so much for his wolfness, but for those of his traits that border on the human.

Let us now skip two generations and listen to the howl of the wolf as heard by Miyax, a young Eskimo girl lost in the

Alaskan wilderness. She is *Julie of the Wolves* by Jean Craighead George, and this is how she assumes the mask of the wolf.

> Miyax pushed back the hood of her sealskin parka and looked at the Artic sun. It was a yellow disc in a lime-green sky, the colors of six o'clock in the evening and the time when the wolves awoke . . . [S]he . . . focused her attention on the wolves she had come upon two sleeps ago. They were wagging their tails as they awoke and saw each other.
>
> Her hands trembled and her heartbeat quickened, for she was frightened, not so much of the wolves, who were shy and many harpoon-shots away, but because of her desperate predicament. Miyax was lost . . . without food for many sleeps . . . and the very life in her body . . . depended upon these wolves for survival . . .
>
> Miyax stared hard at the regal black wolf, hoping to catch his eye. She must somehow tell him that she was starving and ask him for food . . .
>
> She had been watching the wolves for two days, trying to discern which of their sounds and movements expressed goodwill and friendship . . . If she could discover such a gesture . . . she would be able to make friends with them and share their food . . . "*Amaroq, ilaya,* wolf, my friend," she finally called. "Look at me. Look at me."
>
> She spoke half in Eskimo and half in English, as if the instincts of her father and the science of the gussaks, the white-faced, might evoke some magical combination that would help her get her message through to the wolf.

The science of the gussaks and the instincts of her Eskimo father do conspire within Julie; she succeeds in communicating her hunger to the wolves, and they bring her caribou meat.

From Little Red Riding Hood to Julie covers a great interior distance: from being eaten by a wolf to being fed by one.

From inside a wolf mask to inside a wolf's head. The distance is not only great but also deep. Under the wolf mask you might feel close to the wolf, but from these stories, you can feel intimate with him.

Children who have the great good fortune to read, or be read, the books in which these wolf stories are told can know more and fear less than those who sit in the assembly of the tribal elder who has donned the totem mask of the wolf. Books allow us to know the wolf's fierceness and tenacity, yes, but we can also know his loyalty. We can know his pride as leader of the pack, but we can also know his nobility in defeat. We can know more and can imagine more.

When the masks are books, we can pass down to future generations not only the fearsome magic of a single shaman in a totem mask but the richer magic of many. We can pass down a whole trunkful of wolf masks, and we can have them ready in sizes to fit all ages. We can let our children and our grandchildren know the wolf of the many writers who have donned his mask.

—+—

New Orleans is not the only city famous for its carnival. Rio and Venice are famous, too. All three of these cities share an exotic geography—one that is intimate with water—and each has its particular traditions, but whether the festival celebrates Fat Tuesday as it does in New Orleans and Rio or whether it celebrates the Ascension as it does in Venice, all of them celebrate with masks. The festival in Venice is the oldest of the three, and at the time of the Renaissance, when a nobleman pinned a mask to his lapel, it was a reminder to others that he was traveling incognito.

Does making an announcement that you are traveling incognito seem a contradiction of terms? Batman and the

Lone Ranger always did; Romeo wore a mask to the house of the Capulets. Movie stars used to wear dark glasses to indicate that they were traveling incognito. Nowadays, even though sunglasses have become a fashion statement, they still function as a mask of incognito for those of us who are less than celebrity but have run out to the grocery store without makeup—another one of our everyday masks.

Sometimes the choice to travel incognito is not ours to make.

Saturday, 20 June, 1942
I haven't written for a few days, because I wanted first of all to think about my diary. It's an odd idea for someone like me to keep a diary; not only because I have never done so before, but because it seems to me that neither I—nor for that matter anyone else—will be interested in the unbosomings of a thirteen-year-old schoolgirl . . .

. . . I [was born] on June 12, 1929, and, as we are Jewish, we emigrated to Holland in 1933 . . .

After May 1940 good times rapidly fled: first the war, then the capitulation, followed by the arrival of the Germans, which was when the sufferings of us Jews really began. Anti-Jewish decrees followed each other in quick succession. Jews must wear a yellow star . . .

Wednesday, 8 July, 1942
Dear Kitty,
Years seem to have passed between Sunday and now. So much has happened, it is just as if the whole world had turned upside down . . . Margot told me that the call-up was . . . for her. I was more frightened than ever and began to cry. Margot is sixteen; would they really take girls of that age away alone? But thank goodness she won't go, Mummy said so herself; that must be what Daddy meant when he talked about us going into hiding . . .

# E.L. Konigsburg

Thursday, 9 July, 1942

Dear Kitty,

    So we walked in the pouring rain, Daddy, Mummy, and I, each with a school satchel and shopping bag filled to the brim with all kinds of things thrown together anyhow.

    We got sympathetic looks from people on their way to work. You could see by their faces how sorry they were they couldn't offer us a lift; the gaudy yellow star spoke for itself.

The gaudy yellow star was a badge that rendered Anne Frank, her mother, and her father incognito to the point of being nonpeople. They became invisible. And when they lost their mask of invisibility, Anne Frank, her mother, and her sister Margot lost their lives.

*Anne Frank: The Diary of a Young Girl* was not published as a children's book, but children have adopted it. As they read it, they learn not only what it feels like to be incognito but also what it is like to have a long, penetrating look at your inner self because your outer self has been rendered invisible. It is one of those books that youngsters in the fifth and sixth grades reread and re-reread and do so each time with anticipation and discovery.

Saturday, 15 July, 1944

    . . . It's really a wonder that I haven't dropped all my ideals, because they seem so absurd and impossible to carry out. Yet I keep them, because in spite of everything I still believe that people are really good at heart . . .

The diary of Anne Frank is an introspective book, and those fifth- and sixth-graders who read it over and over are introspective readers. It has been my experience that children reread books they love up until they enter the seventh grade. I think there are several reasons why this is so. One reason, of course, is that the assigned reading load becomes heavier in the seventh grade, but there is another, more poetic reason why this is so, and in order to explore it, I must tell you about the Bapendes tribe of the Congo.

Before a Bapendes youth can be proclaimed a man, he undergoes a long ordeal–the details of which I do not know–after which he appears to the elders of the tribe wearing a mask *representing the ghost of his childhood.* I know of only one other elaboration of the ritual of the Bapendes, but I would like to talk about that a little later.

Right now, I want to think about a mask that represents the ghost of one's childhood.

Would you please take a minute to think about making such a mask?

Don't try for a photographic representation of yourself as a child, but try to design a mask of the ghost of your childhood. There is a lot to be decided. What materials will you use? Will your mask be clay or wood or papier mâché? Will the mask of your childhood be pastel or bright? Is it smiling? Is it fat and full or thin and skimpy? Is it knit of yarn of many colors? Is it cast in stone?

This is not an easy assignment. Think about it, please.

Close your eyes if it helps and promise not to cry.

Do you have an image?

Is the mask of the ghost of your childhood still unfinished? We have probably all built the mask of the ghost of our childhood on an armature made from a branch of some family tree, and we have stretched the material of family life over that frame. There are probably holes and patches—quarrels and reconciliations—in everyone's fabric, but I'm willing to bet that every mask is covered with a lacy web of dreams. Dreams of what we will see. Dreams of what we will be. Dreams that must remain on the mask of the ghost of your childhood to help define it. The web of dreams may not be the skeleton of your mask, but doesn't that web hold it together? And make it your very own?

Is there a silvery thread in that web of dreams where you were a knight in shining armor? Is there a sturdy woolen skein where you had a nanny and lived in a proper English household? Did you talk to animals? Were you kidnapped? Were you an orphan growing up in India? Or England? Colonial America? Did you ride an elephant? A river boat? A covered wagon? Did you fly? Did you travel through time? What are the threads of dreams that cover the mask of the ghost of your childhood?

Those readers who are rereading Anne Frank's diary and whose letters tell me that they have reread books of mine are, I believe, gathering materials for their masks. These readers are not sure what materials they need or how much they need, and as they add to and take away, they reread those books that they can mine for raw materials. The responsibility is awesome.

I am convinced that the rereading stops when the material gathering stops and that is the time when the young man or the young woman is asked at last to construct the mask of the ghost of his childhood, and nowadays, that is often at the end of the sixth grade, when the child is twelve.

Being twelve is special. It is the end of childhood, it is the April of our years. April is the cruelest month, and twelve is the cruelest age. It is a watershed in one's emotional development. A wise librarian once told me that if Booth Tarkington were to write *Seventeen* today, he would have to call it *Twelve.* I think that when I was growing up, he would have called it *Fourteen,* and four hundred years ago it would have been *Nineteen.* I didn't pick the number nineteen out of the air.

Recently, I was listening to a radio interview with a director of Renaissance choral music. When asked why he had included female voices even though no women's parts were included at the time the music had been written, the choral director replied that it was necessary to use female voices to achieve the full range of the music. He elaborated by saying that he cannot start training until the age of nine or ten and then, by the age of thirteen, male voices begin to change. Whereas, years ago, when Renaissance music was being written, male voices changed much, much later—sometimes as late as nineteen.

Nowadays, like it or not, twelve seems to be the age at which children carve their masks. It is the age at which the peer group begins to pull—and pull strongly. If that mask is not deeply carved, if it is not made of good material, if it does not have its own contouring veil of dreams, if it is set out and allowed to be painted on or rubbed smooth by peers, it can never, never be really and truly one's own.

Those of us who write for children must give them a variety of masks to try on, and we must write rich and deep so that they can choose what materials they want for the body of that mask. And we must provide threads of many colors to let them weave the web of fantasies to lay over its surface.

*We are such stuff as dreams are made on,* and writers have a great responsibility to provide the raw stuff of those dreams. Writers—unlike producers of television shows or movies—can provide the one ingredient that I offered before when inviting readers to try on wolf masks. And that is intimacy. Intimacy—that degree of privacy that is plural but not public—is the place where we can try on an eccentric mask and, wearing it, pose this way and that. It is the place where we can unselfconsciously shape a dream to make it fit and where we can reject those masks we don't like, for the weaver need never know that we have even tried it on.

> Tuesday, 4 April, 1944
> Dear Kitty,
>     . . . I want to go on living even after my death! And therefore I am grateful to God for giving me this gift, this possibility of developing myself and of writing, of expressing all that is in me . . .

I wish I could tell Anne Frank that she has gone on living. She has helped many children shape the masks of the ghosts of their childhoods.

—✧—

Masks can reveal; they can conceal; but they all exaggerate. And therein lies some of the truths they tell.

Several years ago I wrote a book called *Up From Jericho Tel*. Jeanmarie begins telling her story as follows:

> There was a time when I was eleven years old—between the start of a new school year and Midwinter's Night—when I was invisible. I was never invisible for long, and I always returned to plain sight, but all my life has been affected by the people I met and the time I spent in a world where I could see and not be seen.

Being invisible is, of course, the most exaggerated mask of incognito. Jeanmarie's invisible life begins when she falls into Jericho Tel and meets Tallulah, the ghost of a famous actress, who sits on an enormous sofa piled high with pastel-colored pillows, and who, as Jeanmarie says, "told wonderful stories about the theater, and [who] always had something funny to say."

Jeanmarie wrote down many of the things Tallulah said. At the beginning of chapter 16, this appears:

> Tallulah says, "If you want to learn the difference between accuracy and truth, look at a photograph of Gertrude Stein and then look at Pablo Picasso's portrait of her."

According to *The Autobiography of Alice B. Toklas,* here is a description of how Picasso came to paint that famous portrait.

> [Gertrude] took her pose, Picasso sat very tight in his chair and very close to his canvas . . . and the painting began . . . All of a sudden Picasso painted out the whole head. I can't see you any more when I look, he said irritably, and so the picture was left like that.
>
> Some months later he . . . returned to the faceless portrait and imposed the intense, discordant mask without looking at the sitter. The face clashes against the body to create the picture's grip. This ritual mask has now taken the place of all camera likenesses as our idea of Gertrude Stein.

Picasso said, "We all know that Art is not truth. Art is a lie that makes us realize truth."

Tallulah and Alice B. Toklas would say that the mask delivers a truth that the camera cannot.

There is a point beyond which accuracy does not matter.

My college education and my first work experience were in the world of science, and it was there that I learned the language of millimeters. It is in the world of science that accuracy is most prized, but even in science there are limits. There is, for example, the case of pi. Pi is the constant made famous in sixth grade when we learned that the formula for finding the area of a circle is $\pi r^2$. Pi is the ratio of the circumference of a circle to its diameter. We first knew pi informally as three and one-seventh, and later we got to know it as 3.14159, which we were allowed to round off to 3.1416. At the end of the nineteenth century, an obscure British mathematician named William Shanks—when both calculators and anabolic steroids were unknown—spent twenty years working out pi to 707 decimal places—only to fumble after 527. The 528th decimal place of pi is 4, but Shanks called it 5, and from there on all his digits were wrong. But here's the thing of it: for more than seventy years no one knew that the 528th decimal place of pi is 4 and not 5, and for all those years no one cared.

In 1973, as computers became faster and more sophisticated, a French mathematician calculated a million decimal places. The French, being very proud of this accomplishment, published the million decimal places of pi as a four-hundred-page book. It has never made the *New York Times* best-seller list. By 1988, the Japanese extended that million decimal places to 201 million, and in 1989, David and Gregory Chudnovsky of MIT calculated pi to 480 million decimal places, and a few years later, they made it a billion.

Even the brothers Chudnovsky would probably admit that a billion decimal places of pi don't say too much more than good old 3.1416 did. There is a point beyond which accuracy may have rhythm but no meaning.

The business of accuracy and truth is a tricky one. If you want to see something that is accurate but not true, I would once again recommend Williamsburg, Virginia. There everything is accurately reconstructed down to the last quarter inch. Everything is tied down, wrapped up, a neatly packaged, pretty good imitation of the truth. But that which is exaggerated often tells a greater truth.

The masks, the painted faces, the costumes, the exaggerations of Mardi Gras showed a truth just as the masks, the painted faces, and the costumes do in the theater. In ancient Greek theater, when a player wanted to take on several roles, he would put on a different mask for each role. So that the audience sitting in the back rows would not mistake who was talking, the features of the masks were exaggerated. Even today, in live theater, actors apply makeup that is so heavy it is called greasepaint. And when a civilian appears in makeup that is heavily applied, we call such exaggerated makeup theatrical.

It is the role of masks to exaggerate. Who's to say which is the real Tammy Faye Bakker: the face? or the mask?

As any good humorist will tell you, there is truth in exaggeration.

It has been said that the difference between English and American humor is that the English make the ordinary seem extraordinary, and the Americans make the extraordinary seem ordinary. Both imply exaggeration.

Take this example by a quintessential American humorist, Mark Twain. *A Connecticut Yankee in King Arthur's Court* is about to set out in search of adventure:

> I was to have an early breakfast, and start at dawn, for that was the usual way; . . . my armor . . . delayed me a little. It is troublesome to get into, and there is so much detail. First you wrap a layer or two of blanket around your body, for a sort of cushion . . . then you put on your sleeves and shirt of chain mail . . . very heavy . . . then . . . your shoes–flat-boats roofed over with interleaving bands of steel–and screw your . . . spurs into the heels. Next you buckle your greaves on your legs, and your cuisses on your thighs; then come your back-plate and your breast-plate . . . then you hitch onto the breast-plate the half-petticoat of broad overlapping bands of steel which hangs down in front but is scolloped out behind so you can sit down . . . next you belt on your sword; then you put your stove-pipe joints onto your arms, your iron gauntlets onto your hands, your iron rat-trap onto your head . . . and there you are . . .
>
> Just as we finished . . . I saw that as like as not I hadn't chosen the most convenient outfit for a long trip . . .

Exaggerated understatement renders the extraordinary ordinary and makes it funny. And makes it true. Humor can do what no long, detailed, and accurate catalog of arming a knight ever could.

Fiction delivers. Humor delivers accurately.

—✢—

I mentioned earlier that I know about one other elaboration of the rite of the Bapendes tribe of the Congo. It is this: After the young man passes through the ritual of making a mask of the ghost of his childhood, that mask is cast aside and replaced by a small ivory duplicate, which is worn as a charm against misfortune and as a symbol of his manhood.

Do you carry a small charm of your childhood with you?

It might be a healthy thing to carry a replica mask of your childhood–to polish up every now and then and review the web of fantasies that once you laid down thread by thread.

Does Charlotte write in that web? Does Mary Poppins walk there? Did you ride an elephant with Kim? Do you have a Secret Garden in England? Did you find treasure? Did you float down the Mississippi River on a raft?

In *Up From Jericho Tel,* Tallulah has this to say:

> . . . the camera got harsher and harsher. I have never thought it fair that by the time I could play any age at all–having been through them all–the only thing the camera picked up was an old lady. I'll never forgive the camera for that.
>
> The camera does lie, darlings. It never sees the girl within the woman, and that girl is always there. Remember that, whenever you see an old lady. There's still part of her that is just twelve years old.

The camera lied about Tallulah because it was too literal, too accurate, and could not pick up the replica mask of the ghost of her childhood. The camera cannot scan for it, but we can. If we look, we can find it in a person or in his work. I think

Picasso carried a replica mask of his childhood with him. I think Einstein did, too. The late Nobel Laureate Richard Feynmann did, and so did Nobel Laureate Barbara McClintock. Faulkner did; Hemingway did not. Mozart did; Wagner did not. Early J. D. Salinger did; late Salinger does not. Maurice Sendak: yes, always. Barbara Bush, yes; Nancy just said no.

Walk the beaches in South Florida, and every now and then, you will find a few people wearing masks of wrinkles and gauntlets of liver spots, but who have hidden—out of focus of any camera—the replica masks of the ghosts of their childhoods. They are the ones who can still be astonished, the ones who are still curious and who continue to feel outrage at things other than the high cost of living and the low monthly payments of Social Security. They are the adults with perspective, with humor, and—very often—with a book in their hands. They are the ones who know that they have not been able to wear all the masks they once read about, but they are glad that on the small replica of the mask they carry, there is evidence that—once upon a time—they tried them on.

I am not a poker player, and I cannot marry everyone I really want to know. I cannot take them all to Mardi Gras, either, but I can ask them what children's books they've read. If you really want to know someone, ask him that. Ask him what children's books he's read.

Someone once said, "If I can write all the nation's ballads, I don't care who writes its laws." In this fortunate career I have, I have often said to myself, "If I can write all the nation's children's books, I don't care who writes its laws."

One spring, not too many years ago, I spoke at a children's literature festival in suburban Baltimore. The following day, I was to meet my son Paul at a restaurant in the Inner Harbor. It was early evening when I arrived; shops and offices were closing, and as I walked across the floor of the restaurant to see if I could spot Paul's car in the parking lot, I heard a young man call my name. He introduced himself and told me that he had gone to hear my lecture the previous evening, and I was flattered to learn that he had driven in the rain from Baltimore to the far reaches of its suburbs to hear me. He asked me to join him for drink. As we sat down, he said, "I was in a bookstore some years ago. As I was looking over the shelves of children's books, I saw *Jennifer, Hecate, Macbeth, William McKinley and Me, Elizabeth,* and I said to the young woman standing next to me, whom I didn't know at the time, 'That is my all-time favorite children's book.' She said, 'Mine, too.'" He smiled and added, "I married that young woman."

I know I can't write all the nation's children's books, but I have written some. And that will do. Writing some is a double privilege. Not only do I get to take out that small replica mask of my childhood and pull at the threads of its fantasies and weave them into new ones but also because I have written some, I know that for two young people in Baltimore, Maryland, there exists on the masks of their childhoods a little girl named Jennifer sitting in a tree, and maybe for others she sits there in the divine company of a little girl named Anne Frank, who is more visible in death than she was in life. And for others, maybe not for many—but for some—on the replica mask of the ghost of their childhoods, there is a small stain of another ghost named Tallulah who wants you to preserve the mask beneath your face. And wants you to look for it in others.

And so do I.

# Here in the 90s

Since I wrote "The Mask Beneath the Face," I have learned that one of the masks of the wolf has lost its fangs. In the interest of political correctness, "Little Red Riding Hood" has been rewritten. In the new Golden Books version Grandma does not get eaten by the wolf. (Too much violence. Too much sexual innuendo.) Instead, Grandma hides in a closet, finds some linens and a needle, whips up a ghost costume, comes out of the closet in her ghost costume, scares the wolf, and he runs away.

The anti-ageists will be pleased. The Womyn of Antioch may or may not be: grandma is a womyn hero all right, but she saves her life by sewing—woman's traditional work. And the animal-rights lobby is bound to be very unhappy with the New Wolf. I expect them to demand that wolves write wolf books after all.

Here we are, all of us in the field of children's literature, sitting on the edge of the information superhighway, our VCRs blinking, and the people out in left field are busy putting fig leaves on David.

Don't the politically correct know that it is not nice to correct your elders? Don't the politically correct understand that what the unrewritten classics have to offer is what the naked David has to offer: a record of how a civilization felt about itself at a given time. "Little Red Riding Hood," as written by the Brothers Grimm–politically incorrect, sexy, and scary–is part of my past and my children's past and in a few years I expect it to be part of my grandchildren's past. It is as integral to the culture I want to pass down as how I make my brisket.

Books offer something more than content. They offer continuity of experience, and reading offers a unique process. Reading as a means of processing information is unique to human experience. I would put reading right up there with the opposable thumb, Michelangelo, and milk chocolate in the order of evolutionary milestones. Books establish and reinforce a perception of the world that has gone on for six thousand years. Programming our brains to print is necessary to establishing the continuity of our civilization. But the network of the information superhighway is threatening the program with cancellation.

If we are to save this evolutionary high road, we must start on time. We must start with the children, and therefore, the books we start with must be children's books.

My joy and despair that this is so is the theme I addressed when I delivered the Anne Carroll Moore Memorial Lecture at the New York Public Library in November 1992.

# 9. The Big Bang, the Big Picture, and the Book You Hold in Your Hand

Twenty-eight years ago, two scientists from the Bell Laboratories in New Jersey aimed a radio telescope at the constellation Cassiopeia in order to measure the radio waves coming from there. Instead of getting the clear signal they expected, they got a lot of static. Something was wrong. They checked their equipment and found a pair of pigeons nesting in the horn of the telescope. They removed the pigeons as well as a deposit of some "white dielectric material," but the static persisted.

Since they were taking their measurements from a spot close to New York City, they next wondered if the noise could possibly be coming from the stars of the Great White Way instead of the Milky Way. I hate to say this because I do love New York, but in the universal scheme of things, bright lights, big city cause little static. The buzz persisted.

The scientists found the buzz not only wherever but also whenever they pointed their telescope toward heaven. Throughout the course of an entire year, through one full revolution of the earth around the sun, through four seasons, night and day, day and night, this unexplained noise persisted.

Finally, from a combination of calculation, consultation, and a process of elimination, Arno Penzias and Robert Wilson knew what they had.

The sounds they were hearing were the reverberations of the Big Bang, that cosmic explosion that occurred some 12 to 15 billion years ago . . . that same cosmic explosion that produced every atom on the earth, in the seas, and in the air we breathe. The same explosion that formed every atom in this room, its chairs, and its people. We all came into this world, not with a whimper, but with a bang—a big bang—one that was so loud that it is still being heard billions and billions of years later. Penzias' and Wilson's discovery means that all the sounds made by all the world since time began are out there. When we say "heaven knows," it does.

Think of it. The sounds of the four-year-old Mozart playing the piano and the sounds of Shakespeare acting in his own plays are out there. His voice is out there. And so is Antony's wooing Cleopatra and Moses's receiving the Ten Commandments. And Charlton Heston and Mel Brooks doing the same.

It is all out there. Your baby's first words and what your mother-in-law really said about your brisket, your hemline, and your housekeeping. It's all there: spoken Sanskrit, *Veni, Vidi, Vici,* and "I am not a crook." And so are the sounds of those eighteen and a half minutes of lost tape, and if we had a radio telescope properly aimed and sensitive enough, we could hear it all.

Penzias and Wilson discovered that there is no void in the Great Void, and for their discovery they received the Nobel Prize in physics in 1978.

Twenty-nine years before that, Jorge Luis Borges wrote a story about a man who has an instrument—not to hear everything but to see everything. He called his story "El Aleph."

Borges himself is a character in his story.

He tells of meeting another writer by the name of Daneri who is writing a poem called "The Earth" in which he is setting to verse nothing less than "the entire face of the planet." Borges makes Daneri's work sound like an interleaving of

*Harlot's Ghost* with the *World Almanac,* written in the style of James Joyce—long, long-winded, and inconclusive.

One day Borges gets a call from Daneri, who is very, very upset because his house is about to be demolished. He tells Borges that without his house he cannot possibly finish his epic poem, that very work in which he is setting to verse "the entire face of the planet." Daneri confides that in his house, in the cellar of his house, under the stairs of the cellar of his house, is the Aleph.

"The Aleph?" Borges asks.

Daneri says, "Yes, [it is] the only place on earth where all places are—seen from every angle, each standing clear, without any confusion or blending."

Borges is skeptical but goes down into the man's basement to have a look. As instructed by Daneri, he positions himself under the cellar stairs, counts off nineteen steps, looks up, and sees the Aleph. "I saw a small iridescent sphere of almost unbearable brilliance . . . The Aleph's diameter was probably little more than an inch, but all space was there, actual and undiminished. Each thing . . . was infinite things, since I distinctly saw it from every angle . . ."

I can quote only a small part of the remarkable passage in which Borges tells what he sees as he looks into the Aleph.

> I saw the teeming sea; I saw daybreak and nightfall;
> . . . I saw convex equatorial deserts and each one of
> their grains of sand; I saw a woman in Inverness whom
> I shall never forget; I saw her tangled hair, her tall fig-
> ure, I saw the cancer in her breast . . . I saw the slanting
> shadows of ferns on a greenhouse floor; I saw tigers,
> pistons, bison, tides and armies; I saw all the ants on the
> planet . . . I saw the circulation of my own dark blood; I
> saw the coupling of love and the modification of death.
> I saw the Aleph from every point and angle, and in the
> Aleph I saw the earth and in the earth the Aleph and in
> the Aleph the earth; I saw my own face and my own
> bowels; I saw your face; and I felt dizzy and wept, for

my eyes had seen that secret and conjectured object
whose name is common to all men but which no man
has looked upon–the unimaginable universe.

Borges leaves Daneri's house, rattled by his experience,
"afraid [he] would never again be free of all [he] had seen."

The house is demolished, and the Aleph is destroyed.
Months later, excerpts of Daneri's poem–not the "entire face
of the planet"–are edited and published, and Daneri "no
longer cluttered by the Aleph," wins a prize.

Just as it was paralyzing for Daneri to try to communicate
all that he saw, it would be paralyzing to try to communicate
all that we hear. Imagine the terrible burden of being able to
both see it all and hear it all.

In "Renascence" Edna St. Vincent Millay has this to say
about being omniscient:

> For my omniscience paid I toll
> In infinite remorse of soul.
> All sin was of my sinning, all
> Atoning mine, and mine the gall
> Of all regret. Mine was the weight
> Of every brooded wrong . . .
>
> Ah, awful weight! Infinity
> Pressed down upon the finite Me!

In a word, if our eyes could see it all and our ears could hear
it all, it would be godawful.

We would scream: Give me something, give me an instrument so that I can select what I see and what I hear. And give
me some tools so that I can finely tune and delicately focus it.

The bad news is that there is something that is threatening
us all with omniscience. It is already making us dizzy and we
are about to lose consciousness.

The good news is that each of us already has an instrument
that is wired and properly aimed to let us select, and we

already have tools with which to finely tune it. The instrument we have is the human brain. It comes correctly wired, and the tools with which we can finely tune it are *one,* our need to connect, and *two,* our gift to learn, and *three,* children's books.

You're probably thinking: what a stretch! You're probably thinking: what *chutzpah.* But I want to tell you, it sounds good to me. And, Dr. Seuss and Lewis Carroll, wherever you are, I know it is sounding good to you.

I am convinced that now, in this, the tag end of the twentieth century, not only do children need children's books to fine-tune their brains, but our civilization needs them if we are not going to unplug ourselves from our collective past.

Because we are human we have a long childhood, and one of the jobs of that childhood is to sculpt our brains. We have years—about twelve of them—to draw outlines of the shape we want our sculpted brain to take. Some of the parts must be sculpted at critical times. One cannot, after all, carve out toes unless he knows where the foot will go. We need tools to do some of the fine work. The tools are our childhood experiences. And I'm convinced that one of those experiences must be children's books. And they must be experienced within the early years of our long childhood.

And that is what I want to talk about today: brains and books. Connections within, connections without, connections between.

Let me first talk about our brains as a personal radio telescope. Let me talk first about its wonderful built-in wiring for tuning out the static of our civilization in order to better tune in its symphony.

Let me tell you about Meg.

Meg is my granddaughter who is exactly ten months old today. She wakens in the morning to sounds of her mother and father pounding on the stairs, the rush of water from morning showers and the toilet flushing. She hears her dog

Fidget bark. She hears dishes rattling. On her way to day care, she hears the car motor, the whistle of the wind, and the songs of birds. But what does Meg say, now that she is beginning to talk. She says *mama* and *dada*. She does not make the sound of the car motor or birds chirping. She does not imitate Fidget barking. She says *dada* or *mama*. Not because *mama* comes from Mother Nature but because it comes from her mother and is in her nature. Meg's mother and father help her tease *mama* out of the myriad of sounds that it is in her nature to hear. The sounds—all of them—are in her head. She is programmed to hear rattles, squeaks, barks, and chirps, but when she chooses to speak she selects those sounds that are uniquely human, those sounds that are the beginnings of language.

Think how wonderful that is. I am full of wonder at it. How does Meg know how to tease out of the cacophony of sounds surrounding her, the exact syllables that connect? She knows because, besides being an adorable baby, she is an adorable *human* baby. Her radio telescope is hardwired as a human—not a puppy, not a refrigerator—and when she sends out her first signals, she does so in syllables, not static. She chooses language. Because language connects her not only to her family but also to the family of man.

Meg may be hardwired to hear it all, but she puts some of those sound bites in storage.

She has to.

Just as Daneri's epic poem, setting to verse "the entire face of the planet," was unreadable until someone had edited it, Meg has to edit out some sounds in order to be better understood. As she acquires greater skill at repeating sounds that make syllables, as she continues to tune her personal radio telescope, she will tune out some frequencies altogether. Since Meg's mother, father, and sister Anna plus two sets of grandparents will communicate with her in English, reception on the English-speaking channels will become clearer than any others. As a matter of fact, Meg will begin to tune out other languages and by the time she is an adolescent, she will shut down those foreign networks. She will even pull the plug on some of them. Meg will so effectively tune out the sounds of the four tones of spoken Chinese and so effectively tune out the sounds of French vowels that by the time she is an adolescent she will not only not be able to say them well, she will not hear them clearly. The wires will be left dangling, unconnected to the section of her brain that hears them.

If, on the other hand, Meg were a Chinese baby, hearing three generations of Chinese-speaking relatives, she would pull the plug on the letter *r*. By the time a Chinese baby becomes an adolescent, he has tuned his radio telescope to such a degree that he no longer focuses on the letter *r* at all. He no longer hears its reverberations. If from birth to adolescence, the frequency that leads to the sound of *r* ceases to be tuned in, ceases to be used, that frequency is no longer received.

If after the onset of adolescence, a Chinese child wants to say *r,* and the channel wire has been left dangling, it takes a lot of trial and error to find that wire and pull it out of the tangle of loose ends. It can be found, and it can be reconnected. It's called practice, practice, practice. If the connection is not found until after adolescence, it will never be fiber-optically smooth—there will always be a relay where the wires were taped.

So we have our first example of a critical time. And that critical time is preadolescence.

We are all aware of the disadvantages of hearing only one language in the cradle. We have all heard the very bad accents that result. Many of us have spoken in those bad accents. There is for some—not for everyone but for some—an advantage to pulling the plug on those foreign language frequencies. It was an advantage for Winston Churchill.

# E.L. Konigsburg

> By being so long in the lowest form (at Harrow) I gained an immense advantage over the cleverer boys . . . I got into my bones the essential structure of the ordinary British sentence—which is a noble thing. Naturally, I am biased in favor of boys learning English. I would make them all learn English; and then I would let the clever ones learn Latin as an honor, and Greek as a treat.

That was what Winston Churchill had to say about tuning out the sounds our language does not make.

But even if we are not sacrificing our skills in order to —as Edward R. Murrow said of Churchill—"[mobilize] the English language and send it into battle," we all have to clean up our wiring some.

To some degree or other, each of us aims our radio telescope in such a way that we sacrifice hearing Hints from Heloise in order to better hear the Sermon on the Mount. Leaving some wires unconnected is necessary not only to avoid cross-wiring but also to make our connections more efficient. We leave some wires unconnected in order to reinforce others.

Long ago, when I wrote *From the Mixed-up Files of Mrs. Basil E. Frankweiler,* I was concerned even then about keeping circuits uncluttered. Claudia, the young protagonist of my story, has just told Mrs. Frankweiler, a rich old recluse, that she should want to learn one new thing every day. Mrs. Frankweiler replies:

> I don't agree with that. I think you should learn, of course, and some days you must learn a great deal. But you should also have days when you allow what is already in you to swell up inside of you until it touches everything. And you can feel it inside you. If you never take time out to let that happen, then you just accumulate facts, and they begin to rattle around inside of you. You can make noise with them, but never really feel anything . . .

## TalkTalk

We disconnect in order to better connect.

We are hardwired to communicate, and we eliminate some connections to reinforce others because we need some trunk lines. Trunk lines are more efficient. They take less energy. An adult can get from Aardvark to Zarathustra faster than a kid can because his wiring is streamlined. And those cleaned-up, litter-free trunk lines are the route to being able to concentrate, being able to think conceptually. Yes, it's the old use-it-or-lose-it message, but it is also something more.

Something much, much more.

More than use-it-or-lose-it, in humans the link between use and strength has a quickening pulse. The more a nerve pattern is used, the better it gets. Well-used nerve paths release nerve growth factors that help ensure their survival. The nerve paths we carve out of the morass of gray cells actually trigger their own growth. I cannot draw a computer analogy for this. I cannot draw a highway analogy. I cannot because this process of growth producing its own stimuli is unique to living organisms. Other things wear out with use. But the human brain gets better with use. There is no toaster oven or Cuisinart or Rolls-Royce in the whole wide world that does not wear out with use. There is no computer that gets faster and better with use; it is the human using it who does.

We connect in order to connect.

Even before we start strengthening those trunk lines, even before those brain cells send out nerve growth chemicals, we must turn on the ignition. And—guess what?—before we do, we must jump-start the battery. Consider our capacity to charge and recharge the brain as a storage battery. We come with it already installed but keep it dry until ready to send out its first spark. We add distilled water to loosen those chemicals that will make the current. Consider those first pure sights and sounds as the distilled water we pour into our human storage battery. Even though new and unused, the human battery still must be jump-started. Then those

**176**

nerve growth chemicals kick in and keep the current flowing. But just as a battery is jump-started with its own product, the brain must be jump-started with experience. Even our most basic patterns of consciousness—seeing and speaking—must be jump-started.

There is evidence.

Dr. Patricia Cowdery is a friend of mine who is a retired medical doctor. Before she completed her medical studies, she worked at the Yerkes Primate Lab, which used to be housed in North Florida, where we both live. She told me of an experiment she observed there in the early forties, in those years when animal-rights groups were hardly a cry in the wilderness. Experimenters kept a group of normal chimps in the dark. The technicians who fed, diapered, and mothered the chimps were allowed only a dim red light, one that did not stimulate the retina. For eighteen months, the chimps did not see light.

Then they did.

After eighteen months, the chimps were allowed to see, but they couldn't. They were functionally blind.

Dr. Cowdery tells of dangling a watch on a chain in front of Dixie, one of the female chimps; Dixie did not reach for it as a normally playful chimp would. Dixie was taking pictures, and the film was being developed, but Dixie did not know if she was looking at a watch or the surface of the moon. She could not interpret. Dixie had never learned to organize the world from images. To identify my friend, Dixie had to touch her, sniff her, and listen to her. Pat Cowdery's face, the face of the watch, or the face of the man in the moon were the same to Dixie because the circuitry between sight and sense was never laid out, and the process of stimulation/use/growth-through-use never got under way.

There is a human analogy to this.

A child who has a lazy eye must wear an eye patch over his good eye to force him to use his lazy eye, force him to connect his organ of sight with the site in his brain that lets him interpret what he sees. He must do it by the time he is seven—or he will not see out of that eye any more than Dixie could "see" the watch that Pat dangled in front of her.

The seer must see in order to see, and the speaker must speak in order to speak.

There is an example in the tragic case of Genie, the California child who was kept in silence in a bedroom, harnessed to a potty chair during the day and strapped into bed at night. She was never spoken to; she received no auditory stimulation at all. She was punished if she cried; she was not allowed to make any noise at all; she never spoke. Her rescue did not come until she was thirteen. She couldn't speak. All tests indicated that the mechanism was intact: her hearing, her vocal cords, the left hemisphere of her brain. All were there. But after her rescue, when she was given every opportunity to talk, she learned words—she was anxious to learn the names of things—but she never learned to string words into sentences. Genie was not rescued until she was past the critical time when her brain needed to lay down the path between sound, speech, syntax, and sense. Rescue came too late for Genie. She never learned to organize the world through language.

We need to experience seeing in order to see. We need to experience speaking in order to speak.

A child who does not speak before adolescence will learn words but will not learn language. He can always learn words. So can a chimp. So can a parakeet. But what he cannot learn is language—the patterns of words that convey meaning. The human connective tissue we call language. It is language, not words, that makes us human.

Unlike the battery that can be jump-started at any time as long as it is intact, the human brain cannot be. Unlike the radio telescope, which will always transmit the reverberations from the Big Bang as long as it is correctly wired, the human brain will not. The human brain will not transmit if during a critical period it has not been jump-started. The human needs feedback. He needs to send in order to receive in order to send.

Dixie and the lazy-eyed child and poor, poor Genie are all telling us that this is something more than use-it-or-lose-it. This is something that precedes use-it-or-lose-it. This is something that happens before the Chinese baby loses his *r*'s or Meg loses her French vowel sounds. They are saying that if you don't stimulate the proper nerves within a critical time, those nerve paths don't get laid down at all.

And you can never, never, never connect.

And every piece of evidence points to the critical age being those years—some sooner, some later—but every one of those critical periods happens before adolescence, during the age when the nonsense of Edward Lear is taken seriously.

And that brings me to books. Children's books.

I am convinced there is a critical time for books, too.

Picture books.

Let me tell you when I realized that I was grateful that I had been exposed to picture books at a critical time. I am not even embarrassed to tell you that a lot of them were comic books. As a matter of fact, those comic books helped.

I was in France, sitting inside Chartres Cathedral, the building that Kenneth Clark has described as "one of the two most beautiful covered spaces in the world . . . one that has a peculiar effect on the mind."

Well, it does. For a while I allowed myself to enjoy the emotional impact and the play of light on the patterns of colored glass, feeling as if I were inside a kaleidoscope. That feeling was soon superseded by the feeling that I was like Borges sitting under the stairs looking into the dizzying world of the limitless Aleph. Everything was there, but I couldn't see. I needed to impose some order on this myriad of pieces and pieces of pieces.

I called on some old patterns of organization.

I saw words. I saw a set of windows that had names written beneath them. I could read: David, Solomon, Aaron. I knew David, Solomon, and Aaron. David, Solomon, and Aaron were friends of mine. They were Old Testament names, familiar to a woman raised in a small Orthodox synagogue in Farrell, Pennsylvania, where we were allowed names but no graven images. So I studied those windows. David had a harp. They got that right. Aaron had a plumed rod, the one given to him by Moses. Correct. But who were those people under my friends, David, Solomon, and Aaron? I studied them. I could make out those names, too: Saul under David. Okay. It figures. Jeroboam under Solomon. Jeroboam? A jeroboam is a big bottle of wine.

I needed a guide.

I got one.

Help came in the form of Malcolm Miller, the eccentric Englishman who has devoted his life to Chartres and whose tours have become, by his own admission–*certainly* by his own admission–legendary. Malcolm Miller sorted out the images; he explained the iconography and connected it to the images and the images to one another. Using his pointer from window to window, he told me stories. He made successive the images that had like the Aleph been simultaneous. He did it with language.

And that is when I knew that these windows were pages of a gigantic picture book. These were Bible tales for the illiterate. And then it further occurred to me that if I had been living in the Middle Ages when Chartres was built, if I had been illiterate, I would have sat in that cathedral and told myself the stories of these windows. If I were illiterate, I wouldn't need the written words at all. I could read the windows as well as Malcolm Miller could. Probably better. But being a twentieth-century woman, I needed subtitles–either spoken or written.

By becoming literate, I had forgotten the language of the windows, but hey, those trunk lines were open, and *words* provided the first dangling cord I had reached for. Written language had allowed me to reconnect those patterns in my brain. With practice, I could recapture the stories of the windows of Chartres Cathedral. And the stories in the frescoes of Adam and Eve, God and Noah on the great ceiling of the Sistine, and I could read Theodora and Justinian in the beautiful mosaics of Ravenna.

I was not deprived like Dixie or Genie. I had merely let my *r*'s get covered over with kudzu.

Think about it.

If I were illiterate, and if I had a kind of time that existed for the people who lived when these works were laid down—a kind of time that does not exist in a world where Federal Express is slow and fax is normal—and the shot heard round the world arrives by satellite—I wouldn't need a guide to read the windows of Chartres Cathedral.

*But.*

But, I was once preliterate.

I once had that kind of time.

I was once preliterate and had that kind of time, and I once had adults who gave me the tools with which to see the story of the pictures. And those tools were picture books, and because I had them, I laid down a network inside my head. I laid down the nerve patterns that let me see pictures as symbols and connect them one to another. With help, with training, I was able to clear the entangling debris of words and read those windows.

Sure, I was reading with an accent. Sure, I had to beam my responses through a relay station, but with practice, I got better and better at it.

Think about children, those preliterates, who are the great audience of picture books. Think about what they are learning from reading pictures. Think about how willing they are

**181**

to learn from pictures. Think about the kind of pony express time they have to do it in.

Think about Meg's sister Anna. She is five. She has already been read to a lot. This year we read *Tuesday* by David Wiesner. Anna laughed out loud. "What's so funny?" I asked. Anna pointed to the frog pushing the remote control with his tongue. When there are no words—or very few—Anna is a better reader than her grandmother.

Anna sees the tongues, and Anna sees the toes.

I am talking about sculptured toes.

The sculptured toes of the bronze charioteer.

Let me tell you about the toes of the bronze charioteer.

When I went to Delphi and saw that wonderful statue in the museum there—the charioteer who stands with the bronze reins in his outstretched right hand—the guide asked us to examine his toes. Each was beautifully sculpted. Even though when the statue was intact, a chariot would have hidden the sight of his toes from the viewer, each toe was carved because, the guide explained, "They were made for the gods' eyes." Small *g*. Plural *gods*.

When I read to my grandchildren or when I write and illustrate books for them, I often think that they are like so many small gods. Small *g*. Plural *gods*. They *know* if toes are missing or are not carved with care.

—✦—

I may have lost some of my preliterate patience. I think I have lost a lot of it. I may have lost some of my preliterate awareness of pictures, and sometimes it is hard to find that dangling cord, and my headset does not come with a remote control—you see, I needed the words—but I do find it, and I can always find my way back because I have the circuitry laid out inside my head.

What if I did not?

What if—as a preliterate—I had never been exposed to picture books? Would I ever be able to make sense of the windows of Chartres? What if I had never seen a picture, never seen a two-dimensional representation of a three-dimensional object, would I have ever been able to sort out the windows? No.

No, I wouldn't. I would be like Dixie or Genie, who could not interpret, and not like the Chinese adult, who has merely lost his *r*'s.

Today's kids, today's American kids, may not have an Aleph, and they may not have a radio telescope, but they have something that is close to being a combination of both. And they need help. They need help teasing out those brain patterns that will let them connect to Churchill and the windows of Chartres, to Shakespeare and the Sistine, to Moses and the Sermon on the Mount.

Let us think about a child who is verbal but not yet literate. He is a preschooler in day care. The TV is on. He interacts well with other kids. The TV is on. He has learned his alphabet from "Sesame Street." The TV is on. He has learned his numbers from "Sesame Street." The TV is on. The child sometimes sits and watches it, the TV that is. Sometimes he is not tuned in, but the TV is on, and the background noise, the buzz, persists. There is no void when the TV stays on.

One day he sees Mount St. Helens, Mount Vesuvius, and Madonna erupting simultaneously because now MTV is on. He hears Talking Heads sing. MTV is on.

He sees "the teeming sea"; he sees . . . "daybreak and night-fall"; . . . he sees "convex equatorial deserts and each one of their grains of sand"; he sees "the slanting shadows of ferns on a greenhouse floor"; he sees "tigers, pistons, bison, tides and armies"; he sees "the coupling of love and the modification of death." He has looked upon "the unimaginable universe."

He does not feel dizzy.

I do.

The Aleph had the virtue of being quiet. This is loud. Man, is it ever loud when MTV is on.

I try to connect.

There are the words. The singer is singing words. Words might help. They helped at Chartres. I listen. Maybe the words will help me connect the pictures with the words. I hear words. This singer sings "Shock the Monkey." Those are his words. They are his only words. He says "shock the monkey" regardless of what image is on the MTV screen. The beat doesn't change either. It is loud. Man, is it ever loud when MTV is on.

I cannot connect. My wiring is faulty. I cannot organize the world as it comes to me on MTV.

I wonder if Amy Elizabeth, who is seven, can connect these images and these sounds and these words. Maybe she can. Maybe she can't but doesn't need to because she has connections that give her an order of consciousness that reading gave to me. Maybe.

The child who by the age of seven has seen a lot of TV and a lot of MTV is bound to be wired differently from me.

He may have wiring that I can only dream about. And that's all right as long as he also has been given books.

Suppose he has never been given a book.

Suppose he has learned a lot but none of it has been from books.

Suppose he has never been given a book and then he goes to school.

He is given a book. It is full of pictures. The pictures don't move. There is no beat. It is quiet. Very quiet. There is no sound at all. There are black horizontal lines on part of the page. They are broken lines. They have a name. They are called *text*. They look to him as Chinese looks to me. Abstract patterns.

He is told that he is to learn from this book. Books require participation. He is supposed to look at the two-dimensional pictures and convert them into three dimensions inside his head. The movement has to happen inside his head. The sound has to happen inside his head. He has to make connections between no sound and the sounds inside his head. Later, he will be expected to translate those broken black rows into language—and convert them into sense inside his head.

Well, all right. Where does he go?

I'll tell you where he goes.

He goes to the back of the class.

Way in back.

Way, way in back. In back of all the other kids who have had books in their hands. I'm not talking head start here. I'm talking jump start. He starts way in back of them because they have already made the connections in the hardwiring of their heads. They are already plugged in. They're already on the double-lane highway, ready to roll, and he will have to clear out the kudzu before he can even start his motor.

And he better do it before he is an adolescent because I want to tell you, he's going to read with a bad accent if he doesn't.

How can we expect any child who has been wired by TV to take to books unless we have helped him build in the circuitry? Won't the child who has learned everything he has ever learned from *moving* pictures and loud sound be wired differently from the child who has linear books? A child who knows that he must get it in a flash has a different brain pattern from a child who knows that he controls something better than the remote; he controls the rate at which he turns the pages. He can study any picture for as long as he wants to. He can take his time and count the toes and see if they're all there and if they're all perfectly made.

It will be very bad for us if we lose the ability to get into books. By becoming literate, we have lost a great deal of our preliterate patience, a great deal of our preliterate power to read continuity from pictures that don't move. But having laid down the circuitry, we can reconnect the wires.

There is no doubt that the TV kids entering first grade have their brains wired differently from mine when I started school. I think of those kids watching MTV, and I think that they do have a desktop radio telescope as well as an Aleph. They see it all, hear it all, unrelated, up front, close, in your face. The sounds they hear and the sights they see are perpetual, staccato, and unrelated.

I see the results in the letters I get.

Here's a letter dated September 1992 from Rebecca in Kansas.

> Dear Mrs Kongsburg
> I think that From the Mixed-up Files of Mrs Bazil E Franklen thats a great book. I would like to another book of yours books are so adventuring well at least that. I think that your one of my favorit authers #1. My name is Rebecca and I in 5th Grade Well if you get this letter please write me back Hears my adress.

And there's my despair as a writer.

Borges felt the same despair. Before he describes what he sees in the Aleph, he says:

> . . . here begins my despair as a writer. All language is a set of symbols whose use among its speakers assumes a shared past. How, then, can I translate into words the limitless Aleph? . . . What my eyes beheld was simultaneous, but what I shall now write down will be successive, because language is successive.

Rebecca writes simultaneously and without verbs. Rebecca's language is not successive. We do not share a past. Rebecca does not know that language could connect us across time.

Rebecca does not know that language could connect us across space. Rebecca does not know that once she mails her letters, they are not in Kansas anymore.

Maybe we pre-MTV people appreciate order too much. Maybe the brain patterns of Rebecca's MTV generation will allow them to connect across time and space in ways that don't involve reading. TV and MTV require a different kind of attention, don't they? They certainly require less processing. Since processing itself not only stimulates but also strengthens nerve paths, I wonder how the learning circuits that lead to concentration, long attention spans, and conceptualization in the TV-taught generation will grow. And I wonder how they will ever mobilize the English language.

I think it is a mistake for educators to disregard the nerve patterns that are being laid down by a "Sesame Street" generation, but it is even a worse mistake to lose the circuitry that books lay down. Or never to lay it down. Our present generation will lose touch with the collective past of our civilization as well as an alternate route to the future.

And I will lose the connections that matter most to me as a writer. More than anything I want to connect. I write to connect. I want to connect with readers. I want to connect with readers of the current generation as well as the past. Books bond the reader and the writer, the reader and the read-to, the generation past and the generation future.

In my picture book *Amy Elizabeth Explores Bloomingdale's,* besides the text—which is linear—besides the full-color picture spread—which doesn't move—I have drawn a strip of black-and-white pictures like a filmstrip. It is my hope that these will not only add to the feeling of Amy Elizabeth's being a tourist but also add a dimension to the text. The filmstrip tells what is going on inside Amy's head, and I hope the nascent reader enjoys this early taste of that most important connection that books make: getting inside someone else's head.

Just as I want to connect the child to the page, I want to connect through time. I want to connect the generations through the book. I have not forgotten the teacher, the librarian, the primary caregiver who is reading that book. I put elements in my picture books that make the reading of them amusing to grandmothers. I know grandmothers. Grandmothers are friends of mine. I want to connect with them, through them, and through them to the book to the child.

Someone wrote that in *Amy Elizabeth Explores Bloomingdale's* Amy Elizabeth's remark about "grandmothers and primary caregivers was . . . cynically amusing to adults." I hope so. Sounds good to me. I am an adult. Adults are friends of mine. Then he went on to say, "but when you laugh, don't be surprised if your listeners feel left out of an inside joke."

Beatrix Potter would never have said that.

Beatrix Potter knew that the small-*g* gods who can count the unseen toes behind the wheels of the chariot can hear the amusement behind the spoken word. The listeners won't feel left out. They may interrupt and ask what's funny, and if you really want to connect, you can tell them. Anna helped me. I interrupted and asked what was funny, and she told me, remember?

Don't let the preschooler give up the two-dimensional, the ordered, the linear. It requires a lot, but it has a lot to offer. It has style.

It has meaning.

And it puts him in control.

He controls the rate, the impact, the time.

If I give up the way I am wired, I give up the world as I know it, and that's an investment of a lot of years. I am not asking the MTV-wired kids to give up their hot-wiring or their remote controls, but I am asking them to plug in mine. They may someday sit in another cathedral—maybe even a library—and need to reattach those wires they once long ago allowed to dangle.

—✛—

That same Big Bang that produced the carbon in the diamonds we wear, in the graphite of our pencils, and in the carbohydrates of our cornflakes also produced the carbon in the proteins of which you and I are made. In our most particulate matter, we are—all of us—the stuff of stars. Doesn't that tell us that we are all in this together? People who need people are not the luckiest people in the world. They are all the people in the world, all over the world standing "hand in hand, and one shock of recognition runs the whole circle round."

That is if we don't blow a fuse or pull the plug.

# TalkTalk

As I was growing up, I always had the feeling that I understood a lot more than I knew. When I listen to my grandchildren, I think that they know a lot more than they understand. The difference is exposure. Even before starting school, they see more and hear more than I had as a high-school graduate. Perhaps, saying *over*seen more and *over*heard more is a better expression because they have been exposed to a great panorama on a very small scale. Their big world is a small place—the size of a television screen. My small world was a big place—my neighborhood.

In the first of these talks, my 1968 Newbery acceptance speech, I expressed gratitude for the recognition and acceptance of my books that made a "record of a place, suburban America, and a time, early autumn of the twentieth century."

It is now the tag end of the twentieth century, and experience appears to have moved out of the family home, off the streets of the suburbs as well as the big cities, out of the neighborhood altogether, and into television.

Television cameras are everywhere: on the playing fields, in the courtroom, in Congress, in war zones, in hospital operating rooms. Between then and now the line between watching something happen and watching it happen on TV has become fuzzy.

Television has blurred the line between real and make-believe.

Consider three newspaper items:

The *New York Times,* Friday, June 8, 1973:

> Students at the University of Michigan Medical School will have the choice of listening to a commencement speaker who is an actor in a doctor's role, or one who is a doctor in an activist's role. The medical school has chosen Robert Young as the official graduation speaker. Dissident students have chosen, as a "counter-commencement" speaker, Dr. Benjamin Spock.

Robert Young spoke to the graduating class of the University of Michigan's Medical School not as an actor portraying a real doctor—Banting, who isolated insulin, or Salk or Sabin—he was there as Marcus Welby, M.D. He was there as the fictional hero of a television series. But in 1973, there were apparently enough young doctors who wanted to hear from a real doctor at their very real graduation.

The *Florida Times-Union,* Friday, April 24, 1987:

> Associated Press
> Howie Mandel, who plays Dr. Wayne Fiscus on TV's *St. Elsewhere,* has been scheduled to address the graduating class next year at Tulane University Medical School.
> You were expecting, maybe, Robert Young?

I have been unable to find a reference where the graduating class of the medical school of Tulane also had a "counter-commencement" speaker. I only hope that when he appeared "words [didn't] escape Howie Mandel." I only hope that he didn't open "with a sequence of Howie howling."

In the wake of the first Rodney King verdict, after the riots in south-central Los Angeles, Vice-president Quayle addressed the Commonwealth Club of California.

The *New York Times,* Wednesday, May 20, 1992:

> EXCERPTS FROM VICE PRESIDENT'S SPEECH ON CITIES AND POVERTY
> I believe the lawless social anarchy which we saw is directly related to the breakdown of family structure, personal responsibility and social order in too many areas of our society . . .
> We must be unequivocal about this. It doesn't help matters when prime time TV has Murphy Brown–a character who supposedly epitomizes today's intelligent, highly paid, professional woman–mocking the importance of fathers by bearing a child alone and calling it just another life style choice.

In November 1862, when President Lincoln met Harriet Beecher Stowe, the author of *Uncle Tom's Cabin,* he said, "So you're the little woman who wrote the book that started this great war." Aside from the fact that we know that Lincoln was teasing about Mrs. Stowe starting the Civil War and Quayle was being unequivocal about Ms. Brown starting civil unrest, we know that Quayle could not have put the blame on an author. Murphy Brown doesn't have one. Book characters are made up by authors. TV characters are made up by committees. Murphy Brown is a blend of writers, directors, producers, and the actress who plays her. Like a good bouillabaisse the blend is more identifiable than the ingredients that make it.

Book characters can't breach the line between politics and make-believe. Authors, not their characters, have always stayed the line. (Ask Salman Rushdie.)

The single episode of "Murphy Brown" that upset Vice-president Quayle had 38 million viewers. Imagine! Thirty-eight million people doing exactly the same thing during a single half hour of a Monday night.

A television show that has an audience of only one million viewers for its particular half hour is considered a flop. A book that has a million readers over a year or two years or five years is a hit.

Television would seem to hold all the chips.

But not if we regard as an advantage what is considered a serious limitation in television. No television show with 38 million viewers per half hour can offer what a single book can offer over a lifetime. Many lifetimes. In 1993 we celebrated the one hundredth birthday of *Peter Rabbit*. *Peter Rabbit* may have 38 million readers over a century of time. Think of it! Four generations sharing a single experience–not within a half hour–but within a century.

As the number of years bearing down on the end of our millennium is in single digits, we are promised five hundred television channels before the digits run out. We are also promised that some of those channels will be interactive.

Now, more than ever, television would seem to hold all the chips.

But not if we consider what books mean.

W. H. Auden said, "Rite is the link between the dead and the unborn."

Reading is a rite as well as a right. Reading is the slow-motion experience–the rocking-chair experience. And children's books are the grandmothers' laps we sit in. Books are meant to speak to us, one by one. They are one individual communicating with another. One generation connecting to another. They speak to the ages through the ages. Some of us have probably already forgotten who Drs. Welby or Fiscus were, but none of us has forgotten who Peter Rabbit is. He is. They were.

I see children's books as the primary vehicle for keeping alive the means of linear learning. They are the key to the accumulated wisdom, wit, gossip, truth, myth, history, philosophy, and recipes for salting potatoes during the past six thousand years of civilization. Children's books are the Rosetta Stone to the hearts and minds of writers from Moses to Mao.

And that is the last measure in the growth of children's literature as I've witnessed it—a growing necessity.

# Permissions

# Art Permissions

*Child's drawing* courtesy of E.L. Konigsburg. Henri Matisse, *Visage.* Circa 1948. Aquatint, private collection. © 1995 Succession H. Matisse, Paris/Artists Rights Society (ARS), New York. Art Resource, NY. Fernand Léger, *The Great Parade (definitive state).* 1954. 117¾ x 157½ ins., oil on canvas. Solomon R. Guggenheim Museum, New York. Photograph by David Heald © The Solomon R. Guggenheim Foundation, New York [62.1619]. Wassily Kandinsky, *Composition.* 1915. © ARS. Museum of Fine Arts of the Georgian S.S.R. Tbilisi, Georgia. Erich Lessing/Art Resource, NY. Georges Braque, *Fruit Dish and Cards.* 1913. © 1995 Artists Rights Society (ARS), New York/ADAGP, Paris. Musee National D'Art Moderne, Paris, France. Giraudon/Art Resource, NY. Juan Gris, *The Book.* 1913. Musee d'Art Moderne de la Ville de Paris, Paris, France. Giraudon/Art Resource, NY. Marcel Duchamp, *Bride.* 1912. 35⅛ x 21¾ ins., oil on canvas. Philadelphia Museum of Art, Louise and Walter Arensberg Collection. Marcel Duchamp, *The Passage from Virgin to Bride.* 1912. 23⅜ x 21¼ ins., oil on canvas. The Museum of Modern Art, New York. Purchase. Photo © The Museum of Modern Art, New York. Juan Gris, *The Violin.* Kunsthaus, Zurich, Switzerland, Scala/Art Resource, NY. Pablo Picasso, *Violin and Guitar.* Hermitage, St. Petersburg, Russia. © 1995 Artists Rights Society (ARS), New York/SPADEM, Paris. Scala/Art Resource, NY. Georges Braque, *Man with a Guitar.* 1914. Musee National d'Art Moderne, Paris, France. Giraudon/Art Resource, NY. Georges Braque, *Violin and Palette.* 1909-1910. 36⅛ x 16⅞ ins., oil on canvas. Solomon R. Guggenheim Museum, New York, Gift, Solomon R. Guggenheim, 1937, Photograph by David Heald © The Solomon R. Guggenheim Foundation, New York [FN 54.1412]. Pablo Picasso, *The Violin.* 1914. Musee National d'Art Moderne, Paris, France. © 1995 Artists Rights Society (ARS), New York/SPADEM, Paris. Giraudon/Art Resource, NY. Pablo Picasso, *Ma Jolie (Woman with a Zither or Guitar).* 1911–1912. 39⅜ x 25¾ ins., oil on canvas. The Museum of Modern Art, New York. Acquired by Lillie P. Bliss Bequest. Photograph © 1995 The Museum of Modern Art, New

York. Georges Braque, *The Portuguese.* 1911. Kunstmuseum, Basel, Switzerland. Giraudon/Art Resource, NY. Pablo Picasso, *Man with a Clarinet.* Thyssen-Bornemisza Museum, Madrid, Spain. © 1995 Artists Rights Society (ARS), New York/SPADEM, Paris. Nimatallah/Art Resource, NY. Georges Braque, *Woman with a Mandolin.* 1910. © ARS. Thyssen-Bornemisza Museum, Madrid, Spain. Nimatallah/Art Resource, NY. Pablo Picasso, *The Aficionado.* 1912. Kunstmuseum, Basel, Switzerland. Giraudon/Art Resource, NY. Georges Braque, *Le guéridon.* © 1995 Artists Rights Society (ARS), New York/ADAGP, Paris. Art Resource, NY. Pablo Picasso, *Landscape at Céret.* Summer 1911. 25⅝ x 19¾ ins., Solomon R. Guggenheim Museum, New York, Photograph by David Heald © The Solomon R. Guggenheim Foundation, New York [FN 37.538]. Marc Chagall, *Self-Portrait with Seven Fingers.* Stedelijk Museum, Amsterdam. Henri Rousseau, *The Muse Inspiring the Poet (M. Laurencin and G. Apollinaire).* Kunstmuseum, Basel, Switzerland. Giraudon/Art Resource, NY.

*Life Magazine cover* (October 20, 1972). Photograph by Leonard McCombe. Life Magazine © Time Warner Inc. Doorway from the transept of the monastery church of Moutiers-Saint-Jean, Burgundy. On tympanum, Christ crowns the virgin; statues possibly of Merovingian kings, Clovis (left) and Clothar (right). Gothic style. Stone, originally polychromed. The Metropolitan Museum of Art, The Cloisters Collection, 1932 and 1940 (32.147, 40.51.1-.2). *Adam and Eve,* from The Hours of Catherine of Cleves. The Pierpont Morgan Library, New York, M. 917, p. 138. © The Pierpont Morgan Library 1995. *Mouth of Hell,* from The Hours of Catherine of Cleves. The Pierpont Morgan Library, New York, M. 945, f.168v. © The Pierpont Morgan Library 1995. *Medieval Stained Glass,* thirteenth century. The Dove returns with an olive twig in her beak to announce the end of the Flood. From the Noah Window at Chartres Cathedral, Chartres, France. Erich Lessing/Art Resource, NY. *Engaged capital,* carved in high relief with two crowned heads. (Possibly Henry II and Eleanor of Aquitaine.) Church of Notre Dame du Bourg, Langon. The Metropolitan Museum of Art, The Cloisters Collection, Purchase, 1934 [34.115.4ab]. *Stone Effigy of King John.* Used with the kind permission of the Dean and Chapter of Worcester Cathedral. *Tombs of the Plantagenet Kings.* Richard I the Lionhearted, Eleanor of Aquitaine and Henry II Plantagenet. Gothic sculpture. Abbey, Fontevrault, France. Erich Lessing/Art Resource, NY. *View of the façade,* Notre Dame la Grande Cathedral, Poitiers, France. Giraudon/Art Resource, NY. *Exterior view of the cathedral—façade.* Reims Cathedral, Reims, France. SEF/Art Resource, NY.

Unknown Artist (after Andrea del Verrocchio), *Bust of a Lady.* Plaster and stucco, painted and gilt. The Metropolitan Museum of Art, Rogers Fund, 196 [65.177]. Leonardo da Vinci, *Ginerva de' Benci (obverse).* Circa 1474. 15¼ x 14½ ins., oil on panel. Ailsa Mellon Bruce Fund. © 1994 Board of Trustees, National Gallery of Art, Washington, D.C. Leonardo da Vinci, *The Last Supper.* S. Maria delle Grazie, Milan, Italy. Scala/Art Resource, NY. *Detail of Sforzesca altarpiece—Ludovico Sforza (called "il Moro").* Pinacoteca di Brera, Milan, Italy. Scala/Art Resource, NY. Leonardo da Vinci, *Cecilia Gallerani (the "girl with the ermine").* Oil on walnut, Muzeum Narodowe Biblioteka Czartorysich, Cracow, Poland. Erich Lessing/Art Resource, NY. Gian Cristoforo Romano, *Beatrice d'Este.* Marble bust. © Réunion des Musées Nationaux. Leonardo da Vinci, *Portrait of Isabella d'Este.* Drawing, Louvre, Paris, France. Scala/Art Resource, NY. Leonardo da Vinci, *Due teste num. 423.* Gabinetto dei Disegni e delle Stampe Firenze. Scala/Art Resource, NY. Leonardo da Vinci, *St. John the Baptist.* 1513–1515. Louvre, Paris, France. Erich Lessing/Art Resource, NY. Leonardo da Vinci, *Mona Lisa.* 1503 and 1506. 77 x 53 cms., oil on panel. Louvre, Paris, France. Erich Lessing/Art Resource, NY.

*Drawings of masks* courtesy of E.L. Konigsburg.